New titles in the Torchwood *series from BBC Books:*

Long Time Dead *by Sarah Pinborough*

First Born *by James Goss*

The Men Who Sold the World *by Guy Adams*

TORCHWOOD
Long Time Dead

Sarah Pinborough

3 5 7 9 10 8 6 4 2

Published in 2011 by BBC Books, an imprint of Ebury Publishing.
A Random House Group Company

The Random House Group Limited Reg. No. 954009

Addresses for companies within the Random House Group can be found at
www.randomhouse.co.uk

A CIP catalogue record for this book is available from the British Library.

ISBN 978 1 849 90284 7

The Random House Group Limited supports the Forest Stewardship
Council® (FSC®), the leading international forest certification
organisation. All our titles that are printed on Greenpeace approved
FSC® certified paper carry the FSC® logo. Our paper procurement
policy can be found at www.randomhouse.co.uk/environment

Editorial director: Albert DePetrillo
Editorial manager: Nicholas Payne
Series editor: Steve Tribe
Cover design: Lee Binding © Woodlands Books Ltd, 2011
Production: Rebecca Jones

Printed and bound in Great Britain by CPI Cox & Wyman, Reading, RG1 8EX

To buy books by your favourite authors and register for offers,
visit www.randomhouse.co.uk

For Kelly and Noah

John Blackman cursed quietly as he crouched to get past a fallen concrete strut and some dangling wires hanging from the collapsed ceiling. Then he cursed again – internally this time – for getting his visor more steamed up than it was already.

He hated the suit. It was claustrophobic and, no matter how cold the actual temperature, there was something about the rubbery fabric that always left his skin and clothes underneath soaking in sweat. That's what he told the rest of the team as he stripped off at the end of the shift. When he was having a quiet, honest-with-himself moment, he knew it was more likely to just be good old-fashioned fear that left him dripping unpleasantly and adding hugely to his washing pile.

He hated being part of the recovery team. He was a scientist. He'd always worked in labs, and had been very pleased with that arrangement. Finding himself assigned to the Department and suddenly in the field wasn't his idea of fun. It wasn't as if he could analyse how anything worked from within the stupid suit and clumsy gloves, so why didn't they just set him up in a nice mobile unit on the surface and he could work there? Most of the equipment and other strange items they'd found had been shattered or broken or apparently useless anyway.

The whole project seemed like a waste of time, but no one argued with the Department. Especially not a science nerd seconded from the laboratories. He'd thought about it once or twice – *more* than once or twice – about going straight up to Commander Jackson and telling him exactly what he thought about this assignment. He'd practised the speech every time he pulled the suit on and made another treacherous journey underground, but somehow the words just couldn't get out of his head. Every time he'd seen the Commander's hulking figure, he'd found that his feet just scurried him on past and his head stayed down. Confrontation had never been one of his strong points. He waved his heavy-duty torch this way and that to check his footing and then edged cautiously onwards into the bowels of the ruined building.

He'd been dreading this part of the job. A lot of the debris on the surface had been carefully cleared away, but the further down they excavated, the more perilous the job became. He could almost feel the weight of the broken building above him, each piece held up precariously by the one next to it, a house of heavy cards ready to crash down on him should he trip and knock one out of alignment. He tried not to think about it. He tried to focus on the job at hand like the Department men did, but it was bloody difficult.

His shirt was already sticking to his skin, and the side of his head itched where his dandruff had come back. So much for not thinking that the place could collapse at any moment. Somewhere over to his left he could hear someone carefully sifting through the rubble, and it calmed him slightly to be reminded that he wasn't alone down here with only the sound of his own breathing being amplified in his helmet. His feet felt firmer on the slightly cleared route down towards the lower level, and he tried to feel more confident. The sooner he got down there and looked around, the sooner he could get out. He'd said he'd take Lucy Waters from the admin section out for a drink tonight. That wasn't helping his sweating situation either.

When she'd asked him if he'd like to go out – two whole days ago now – he'd at first thought it was something of a joke. It wasn't as if Lucy Waters was some kind of Angelina Jolie or anything (he'd probably die if he ever found himself in the same room as a woman like that), but she was well out of his league. A little mousy perhaps, but she had a nice figure and although she always wore prim blouses it was very difficult to not notice her breasts. They were very much in the room, as he'd heard people say.

He, however, was a self-confessed geek through and through. A dislike of vegetables mixed with spending most of his waking hours indoors and away from fresh air had made his skin pasty and slightly flaky, and his thin body never quite sat right in clothes that were always too big or too small. When not in his lab coat, the shoulders of his jackets and shirts carried a dusting of dandruff, and his teeth were slightly yellowed by a dependence on coffee. He'd looked worse as a teenager thanks to several unfortunate bouts of what the doctor described as 'nervous acne'. John had thought the spots were more angry than nervous, and they had left their battle scars around his chin.

All of this, and his primary interests of astronomy, mathematics and video games, meant that John Blackman had reached the ripe old age of 28 without ever having had a proper girlfriend. In fact, John Blackman hadn't even been kissed or grabbed a feel of anyone's tit. But now, he thought, as the air cooled around him and he climbed carefully down into the newly opened up area, all that might change.

Lucy Waters had actually blushed when she'd asked him about the excavation work and how potentially dangerous it was. She'd wanted to know *all* the details, and she'd leaned in close enough that he could smell her perfume on her skin. Excited as he'd been at the time – and had been for the two days since as the number of tissues now littering the space under his bed could testify – he was now absolutely terrified. If he'd had to choose between this strange building collapsing on him or making conversation with Lucy over a glass of wine, he'd have said the two were equally unappealing. But still, he thought, frowning slightly as he dropped through a narrow gap and into the heart of the lower level, if the suit made Lucy Waters horny for him, then maybe he should wear it on the date. At least she wouldn't see how petrified he was then.

He paused as silence closed in around him again, the rest of the men working too far away to hear. As the cold stench hit him, all thoughts of Lucy Waters and her breasts evaporated. What was that? Something foetid; damp and rotting. What had been kept this far down in the earth beneath the thriving social hubbub of Cardiff Bay? He was working here – in fact, risking his life here no matter how much the Department operatives laughed at that suggestion – and all he knew was that it had been some kind of secret government research centre. Even crumbled and wrecked as it was, John knew it had been way more sophisticated than his lab was. It was like a contradiction.

They'd pulled bits of equipment out of here that were made out of metals that were entirely unidentifiable, along with several battered pizza boxes and an old Rubik's cube. The people that had worked here, whoever they were, might have been scientists like him, but he figured they were definitely the trendy variety. They got laid. For a brief second he felt a moment of jealousy and then it was gone. Had they been inside when the building collapsed? They might have been cool, but they were very likely to be dead.

He breathed in short shallow bursts, doing his best to avoid the awful stench, and as he crept forward his foot banged into something hard in the darkness. The metal thump sang out, and he shone the light downwards. He stumbled back slightly. It was some kind of steel drawer and he crouched beside it, stumbling backwards when he saw a human hand. So this was where the stench was coming from. The drawer was open on its side, other pieces of debris littered on it. He swung the torch upwards. What had once been a bank of some kind of steel lockers was now squashed to half its height with the weight from above, and where it had bowed in the middle all its secure contents had shot outwards. For the first time, he realised that perhaps there were worse ways to go than being crushed to death. What else had been stored here with so much security? Chemical weapons? Viruses? The Department had been very quiet on those subjects when he'd asked about the dangers of this job.

He looked down again. What kind of deaths meant people couldn't be buried by their families? He didn't want to be here. Not at all. Not even a feel of Lucy Waters' breasts – any breasts for that matter – was worth it.

He almost shrieked when a low moan interrupted his thoughts. He spun around, waving his torch madly. The noise had come from somewhere to his right. He took a deep breath to calm his racing heart, and listened again. For ten seconds there was nothing, and then there it was:

a soft, wet sound. Feminine. Debris shifted and the moan came again.

'Hello?' he said, softly. The word was deadened by the cold and concrete. 'Is someone there?' The moan came again. Slightly confused, John picked his way towards the source. It couldn't be a survivor. Unless there was a supply of food and water down here, they'd have been dead long ago. Could one of the team have come down here ahead of him and injured themselves?

He raised his hand and clicked the radio button in the side of his head. 'Um, this is Blackman? Down in the vault? I think I've found something?' Static fired back at him. Great. Just what he needed. This was government equipment. How could the radio stop working? It didn't fill him with the greatest confidence. There had been men working at the next level up and he almost called out to them, but the fear of bringing the whole place down on his head kept him quiet. He'd check out whoever was down here, and then go for help. Simple as that. And on the upside, it might get his shift over more quickly.

The moaning sounded stronger, as if perhaps whoever was there was slowly coming round after being knocked unconscious. It was definitely a woman too, which was odd, because he hadn't noticed any in the morning's team. He must have missed someone during his daily battle with his nerves as he got his suit on.

'I'm here,' he said, peering into the darkness and trying to make out where she lay. The torch finally found her, a few metres ahead of him, the bottom half of her body obscured by the top of another of the broken steel drawers. The way she was lying made it look as if she'd crawled as far out of it as she could before losing her energy. That was ridiculous, of course. It must have fallen on her. She couldn't have come out of it. Could she? His mouth dried slightly, and then, as he got closer, she came fully into view.

The first thing he noticed was that she was beautiful. Even covered in dust and with the white smock she was wearing tugged this way and that and her thick, dark hair a messy fan beneath her head, she was absolutely stunning. She sighed again and, as he crouched beside her, he glimpsed the tops of her smooth brown thighs. He licked his lips slightly. That was when the second thing dawned on him. She wasn't wearing a suit. If she was part of the team, she'd be wearing a suit. Where was her suit?

He didn't have time to consider an answer for that before he noticed something strange under the smock, just about where her stomach was. Something was glowing. There was a circle of red pulsing light showing through the fabric. He touched it gently, but all he could feel was her skin underneath. That was wrong. That was definitely wrong. He looked back at the twisted metal and the way she lay, and he knew, as his bladder contracted, that his first impression had been right. She'd come out of the drawer. Had it been her coffin? That wasn't possible, surely?

Her back arched suddenly and she gasped loudly, sitting bolt upright with a sudden jolt. The speed of her movement surprised John, and he tumbled backwards from his crouch into a sitting position.

'Who are you?' he breathed.

She moved like a cat, quick and flexible, and within a second she was free of the drawer and holding his head in her hand. Had she even been hurt at all? Had the moaning simply been a lure? Why was he suddenly so terribly afraid?

He looked up at her face. A small smile teased her full lips as she tilted her head and leaned in towards him.

'I have something to show you,' she whispered. And then she did.

As he looked into the terrible, empty blackness of her eyes, John Blackman knew with certainty that there would never be a date with Lucy Waters. Terror gripped his soul and the darkness that swirled in her eyes sucked him in.

He was so lost, he barely felt it when Suzie Costello stabbed him hard in the liver with a broken shard of glass, all the time smiling at him as he died.

Chapter One

Detective Inspector Tom Cutler wasn't quite sure how he'd ended up back at the excavation site this morning, but somehow here he was. He sipped his cooling coffee and watched for any sign of activity from beyond the barriers. He should have been at the station. He had the paperwork on the Frame case to finish up, and the DCI's weekly briefing was due to start at ten. If he was going to make that, then he needed to leave now. His feet didn't move though. Just five more minutes.

It was barely a month since a terrorist attack had demolished the heart of Cardiff Bay, leaving a bomb crater where the millennium water tower had once stood. When the government teams and the army had first started to dig through the rubble, the crowds had been quite large, mainly muttering about why on earth all the men and women were in protective clothing if the public announcements were to be believed and there was nothing for the residents of Cardiff Bay to fear.

Now, however, they were three weeks in, and most passers-by barely glanced at the Portakabins and sheets of plastic that covered the entrance to the site. There were still army officers guarding the barriers, but there was no real threat of anyone trying to break through. Not since the drunk teenagers had tried to get in on the first weekend of the excavation project. They hadn't succeeded. Cutler and his new sergeant, Andy Davidson, had responded to that call-out from the army and had given the kids a stern warning then taken them home. Cutler remembered that night. Sergeant Andy had done most of the talking. Cutler hadn't been able to take his eyes from the sheets of white plastic. They flapped in the breeze and he caught glimpses of the dark within. It teased him.

The next day had been a day off, and he'd treated himself to lunch in the Bay. He'd eaten quickly and then wandered down to the site, convincing himself it was just a whim, and that it hadn't been the sole purpose of his lunch out. Since then, he'd found time to be here at least once every couple of days. More recently though, his visits had become twice a day where possible. And he was intent on making it possible. Something about the place fascinated him, and he couldn't figure out what it was. When he was away from the site, it was as if he had a quiet itch constantly in his brain.

There was something about this place that niggled at him. As if there was something he should *know*, but every time he went to the place in his mind that was bugging him, there was just an empty space. It was weird. It wasn't like him either. He was the golden boy of the Force and had been ever since he'd solved the now infamous gruesome murders during the Welsh Amateur Operatic Contest and been persuaded to stay in Cardiff rather than head back to London. He was easy-going and got on with all his colleagues, commanding respect where it was due. This solitary behaviour wasn't in his nature.

That hadn't stopped him coming down here *again*, though, and, when he was here, the strangeness of his new obsession didn't matter. He wasn't getting any answers by watching, but he still felt soothed. He shoved his hands into his pockets and frowned. What was that? He pulled out the rectangular packet. Cigarettes? He stared, surprised. When had he bought those? He hadn't smoked in months, and he'd quit so naturally that he found it hard to remember ever being a smoker in the first place. Smoking, like these visits, wasn't in his nature. He went out for long runs at least three times a week and ate healthily. Cigarettes didn't fit with that lifestyle.

Still, as he stared at the packet, he fought the urge to open it and light one up. He shoved them back into his coat; out of sight, almost out of mind. He should leave. He'd be late. He was about to reluctantly turn away when a figure emerged from behind the heavy plastic sheeting. Tom Cutler moved closer to the barriers, wanting to catch a glimpse of the face through the plastic square, but sunlight bounced off it, spoiling his view. Whoever it was nodded a swift hello at the soldier guarding the entrance and then strolled away.

Instead of going into one of the Portakabins, the figure walked straight out through the barriers, barely three or four metres from where Cutler was standing, picking its pace up to a brisk walk. Cutler frowned again. Outside the barrier? In a contamination suit? They never did that.

The figure was pulling off its helmet when sudden activity back at the site distracted Cutler. Another two suited-up people emerged from behind the plastic, but this time they were moving with purpose. They jogged over to the largest of the trailers and ran inside. Cutler glanced back the other way, but the original figure had disappeared. Something was wrong. Had they found something in the site that had freaked one worker out and made them flee the site? That didn't ring quite true. The person hadn't been running. They'd just simply walked confidently away.

He wondered why it bothered him. For all he knew, the restrictions had been lowered and it was fine to leave the site with all the gear still on. He knew nothing about the operation – no one did, even though Commander Jackson had been quite high profile amongst the press and local dignitaries, including coming to their police dinner as a guest of the Commissioner. He was everywhere, but saying nothing of significance. Cutler wondered if anyone else had noticed. But then, no one else appeared to share his fascination with this place.

Back behind the barrier, the figures re-emerged from the cabin. Commander Jackson, in his full army uniform rather than a protective suit, was with them. If his face was anything to go by, then whatever had sent the two men scurrying to find him, wasn't good.

Cutler's phone was ringing. Shit, it was 10.15.

'Where are you, boss?' Andy Davidson asked. Cutler could hear his concern. He was never late – not for a briefing.

'Sorry, I'll be there in five.'

Jackson and the two men vanished behind the plastic sheeting.

'Everything all right, is it, sir?'

'Yeah. Just overslept. Forgot to set my phone.' It was a lousy excuse and he knew it, but Davidson wouldn't question him. His behaviour might have been a bit strange recently but not enough to warrant any probing from either his sergeant or his boss. Not yet anyway. Reluctantly, he turned away and dumped his cold coffee in a bin. It was time to get back to the daily grind. He forced himself not to peer over his shoulder for one last look. He did have *some* control, after all.

'What the hell happened here?' Commander Jackson crouched by the body. 'He's a bloody civilian.'

'He signed a disclaimer. There won't be any trouble.'

Commander Elwood Jackson looked up. Sometimes he wondered just how depersonalised his special detail were. Where did they train them? As far as he was concerned, a little heart went a long way, even in the business of kill or be killed. It was a different Army from when he'd joined up, and when he looked at this new breed – those now siphoned off to be Department men – he felt every year of the passed time in his bones. Not for the first time since he'd arrived in Cardiff, he wondered if he was simply getting too old for all this.

'A man's dead. There already *is* trouble.' The lab rat, pathetically dressed in only his underwear, was lying on his side, and Jackson carefully rolled him over.

'Jesus.' The voice behind him muttered. Maybe these men weren't so inhuman after all. 'What the hell happened to him, sir?'

John Blackman's eyes were bleeding. Commander Jackson couldn't be sure, but it looked very much like they had exploded. A thick piece of glass was also stuck so deep into the dead man's side only a small edge was visible. That wound, however, was clean. It was as if all the blood in his body had been sucked up to his brain and forced out through the terrible injury to his eyes. He swallowed his disgust. This wasn't good.

'He'll have to stay here until tonight. We can get the body out then. Too much of the site is visible to risk it now.'

'What did that to him, sir?'

'Search this area. Look for any device he may have touched or activated by accident.' Commander Jackson looked at poor Dr Blackman's eye sockets again and suddenly felt naked without a suit on.

'And where the hell are his clothes and his suit?' he asked. 'I presume he was wearing clothes under it?'

'I'll check, sir.'

On his feet, Jackson scanned the area with his torch, professionally covering the ground with the light, careful not to pass over anything or miss a space out. Nothing. No sign of either clothes or suit. Metal gleamed in several places amidst the wreckage and he stared at one of the large objects. A large metal drawer. Looked unpleasantly like it might have served as a coffin. No wonder this basement level was filled with the stench of death and rot. He had been warned that they might come across the dead amidst the treasures the Department wanted. And here they were. One drawer nearby had broken open but he couldn't see any glimpse of a body. He looked back down at Blackmore's terrible corpse. Suitless. An empty drawer and a missing suit.

'I need to go and call this in,' he muttered, aware of the two men watching him impassively. He couldn't show any hint of being in any way unsettled by this discovery. They relied on him to stay calm. 'Find that suit. And I want to know if anyone is missing.'

Back in the bright light of his makeshift office, Commander Elwood Jackson couldn't shake off the chill and stink of the vault. There had been a moment's hesitation at the other end of the phone when he'd described the scene to David Elliott, the smooth and calm Department chief he was responsible to, and it hadn't reassured him. The idea that something had got out of one of those broken drawers, killed John Blackman and stolen his suit in order to get away should have been preposterous.

When he'd taken command of this operation it had been made very clear that they were not looking for survivors. Broken down to basics this was an equipment salvage operation. It was simply that the equipment might be highly sophisticated and like nothing Jackson and his men had seen before. That hadn't concerned him at the time. He was used to simply managing operations and following orders from above. That the orders were coming from the Department rather than military command was really neither here nor there. The outcome was the same, and it wasn't as if they were in the field. The building collapsing aside, there should have been no real reason for anyone to be injured or lose their lives. All the men on site knew that whatever they pulled out of the rubble had to go to Blackman and his ilk for further studying. Soldiers, in the main, weren't a curious bunch. That's what made them such good soldiers. No one who ever questioned too much would go and die for someone else's policies. Commander Elwood Jackson had always been a good soldier. He didn't ask questions. He blinked and behind his own eyes he saw Blackman's wrecked ones. A radio buzzed on his desk.

'Yes?'

'No sign of his suit, sir. We'll keep looking.'

'Any personnel unaccounted for?'

'No, all present and correct, sir.'

He turned the radio off and leaned back in his chair. Unease settled like grease in the pit of his gut. He'd learned long ago to trust that feeling. Something wasn't right here. He thought of Blackman's dead body. The missing suit. But most of all he thought about that tiny moment of hesitation before David Elliott had spoken.

Chapter Two

Suzie Costello had dumped the helmet in a passing bin and then stripped the suit off as soon as she found a suitable empty side street. She shoved it behind some overfilled bins and then headed towards the burger bar on the main road. The man's clothes were slightly baggy, but he'd been a skinny little thing and had at least been wearing a belt, which now held his trousers on her hips. The tang of sweat coming from the shirt was unpleasant, but she had no choice but to put up with it – at least for now.

Some people had stared at her as she'd strode away from the Torchwood Hub's wrecked site, but she didn't need to worry about them ever giving a description of her. It was the suit they'd been looking at, not the person inside it.

Inside the fast-food restaurant she took the stairs two at a time and went into the toilets. It was only just gone 10 a.m., and the place was empty. She filled the sink with warm water and began splashing her face with it, washing away the dust and grime that coated her skin. When she was done, she straightened up. The water felt good. Refreshing. It made her feel alive. She *was* alive. She giggled aloud at that, the sound echoing eerily in the small confines.

When she'd first woken up on the floor, she'd simply wanted to get away. She hadn't even known who or *what* she was until she'd been striding away. She had been operating on instinct. Hers and something else's. The more she'd recovered her own memories, the more she'd realised that perhaps she wasn't quite alone in her body. She'd killed the man in the vault – and yes, that had been fun as well as necessary – but it hadn't been entirely her.

Still, she thought, smiling at herself in the mirror. Figuring that out could wait. Torchwood was gone, and she was alive. Now *there* was a turn-up for the books. They could shove that in their smug pipes and smoke it. Their faces rose up behind her eyes, memories she couldn't suppress: Ianto the puppy, Toshiko the repressed, Owen the playboy, Gwen who was everyone's favourite new girl, and then of course, Jack. Her smile twisted into an ugly grimace. They hadn't done so well without her, had they? Maybe if they hadn't been so high and mighty, they'd still be eating pizza and drinking coffee in the Hub. As it was, she wondered if they were even alive?

Anger surged inside her, rage and hurt at those she'd once worked with, and she swallowed it down. She was back. She didn't need them. They could go to hell as far as she was concerned, if they weren't already there. She thought of the nothing she'd been lost in and shivered slightly, despite the warmth. In the mirror, her reflection stared back and her confidence wavered slightly as she raised one hand to touch the back of her head. There was no blood. No exploded skull. She checked once again under the shirt for reassurance. No bullet wounds there either. Not even a single scar to show where Jack Harkness had emptied his gun into her. Why the hell wasn't she in pain? Still damaged? She had been brought back from the dead once before, but it hadn't been like this. This time she was healed, as well as breathing. She looked back into the mirror. This time she really had been *reborn*, not just brought back to life. This was a whole new Suzie.

She needed to do something about her hair. Lighten it, perhaps. Cut it, definitely. It wouldn't take much to change her appearance enough to put anyone off her trail should they come for her. Not that she thought they would. After all, she was dead, right? Twice over? The only people who might think to look for her were Torchwood and, judging by the state of the Hub, if they weren't dead themselves they had to be in too much trouble to be thinking of her. She was a ghost. She giggled again and had to put her hand over her mouth to stop it developing into a full-blown laugh. She had things to do. This was no time for fun. The smile fell away.

Only when she pulled the door open did she see the small sign on the back. *This toilet was cleaned at 8.30 a.m*. The time had been filled in with a wipe-clean marker pen, and next to it were initials and then a date. It was the last two digits that stopped her for a moment. That long? She'd been dead for *three years*? Her teeth gritted and her anger cooled into something else as the memory gripped her. Emptiness filled her vision. The final instant of terrible fear that came with a last breath. *Death*. She hated it. She wouldn't go back to it. She drew in a long, defiant breath. She would *become* it.

'Box 321, please.'

'Certainly, madam.' The prim, middle-aged woman behind the counter smiled up at her. 'If you could just sign in.'

The formalities done, the assistant retrieved the keys and unlocked the gate to the racks of safety deposit boxes in the narrow room beyond. She moved with precise efficiency to the right one, unlocked the housing and took out the metal box from within. She smiled again, and led Suzie to one of the small rooms at the side.

'You'll have privacy there, Mrs Bunting. Let me know when you're done.'

Her key for the box had been taped under a pew in an old church not far from the centre of town. If it had been missing, she wouldn't have panicked – there was always a way into something if you really wanted it – but it turned out that whichever old ladies were responsible for keeping the wooden benches of St Mark's clean, didn't stretch to cleaning underneath them, just as she'd suspected. She smiled, pleased with herself. There was nothing like forward planning.

She emptied the box, shoving its contents into her pockets. A passport in the name of Sue Costa; bank and credit cards in the same name; flat and car keys. A whole new life was waiting for her. The last item in the box made her smile. A knife. Just in case she got here and needed a weapon. Perhaps she should have left a gun in there instead, but a knife was quieter when you needed to get away fast. She turned it this way and that, letting the steel shine. There was something about a knife that she found reassuring. You had to get in close to use a knife. You had to look right into their eyes as that moment of terror struck. You delivered death personally with a knife.

She held the weapon up, like a band across her eyes and staring into their own brown pools of anger, distorted slightly by the metal, she felt the first wave of something strange inside her. She gasped slightly as something looked out through her eyes and she, in turn, looked back into something. Something terrible. It was beyond the black nothing of death. It was something totally *other*. Something cold and awful – a space between dimensions. And it wasn't empty. Her ears throbbed with the echo of distant sobbing and she knew – although she didn't know how she could possibly know – that it was the man she'd killed in the vault that she could hear. The darkness – this *living* darkness – tugged at her and she gasped again, lowering the knife. Where the hell had that come from? What was it? And how was it connected to her?

She took a moment to regain her breath, letting heat and life flood back to her cheeks. The answers could come later, when she had time to think. There would be an explanation. There always was.

Slowly, she cooled down. *It's hungry. It wants me to feed it.* The thoughts came from nowhere, but slowly Suzie smiled again. For now, it was all she needed to know. It was hungry, and she was angry. She'd felt the terror of the moment of death twice too many times. It was time she shared it. Maybe if she shared it enough, it would leave her alone. One thing the reborn Suzie Costello was sure of – she had no intention of dying again. She tucked the knife into the back of her trousers.

'All done?' the assistant was sitting back behind her desk when Suzie emerged, but was straight up on her feet. She was in good shape for her age, Suzie thought, as she approached. She looked like a runner. Sleek limbs. Toned skin. Put her in some different clothes and she'd probably pass for 40. Not that that would be happening any time soon. Any time at all, in fact.

'Yes, thanks.' Suzie smiled as she handed over the box. When the woman had taken it, and her hands were full, Suzie gripped her arm. Something shifted inside her. The empty universe so far removed from this one yawned greedily behind her eyes. Her smile widened as the assistant's fell.

'I have something to show you,' she whispered. The woman's alarmed gaze met her own unnatural one, and she slumped in her grip. The moment was nearly here. Suzie smiled and pulled the knife from the back of her trousers.

She was still smiling as she lay in the bath two hours later. She'd forgotten how good killing felt. Perhaps she'd just never admitted it to herself before. But that had all been before the darkness. Before she had become *Death* itself. Now she was just doing what was in her nature. The water was hot, and it was good to be warm. She pushed the bubbles around and then sat suddenly upright as something beneath the surface caught her eye.

The red light flashed under the skin of her stomach. Her mouth fell open. So that was it. Suddenly it all made sense.

Chapter Three

'Where did you say you found it?'

'It was on the beach. My trousers are ruined.'

'You wanted to try some fieldwork, Ianto,' Suzie smiled. 'Maybe buy some cheaper trousers if you want me to send you out again.'

'It was hardly fieldwork. Picking up a piece of recovered tech.' Ianto sipped his coffee.

'True. But you're not the only one in expensive trousers, and the signal was coming from the beach, and I'm the boss.' She smiled again, and then focused on the item on the table.

'Any clues yet, Tosh?'

The item was the size of a credit card but made of some kind of metal with three clear stones of some variety embedded in it.

'No. I can't see how to activate it, at all.' The Japanese woman peered through her thick glasses and then lifted the item again. 'It's heavier than it looks.'

'Yes, I don't need you to state the obvious. Maybe when Jack and Owen get back, they'll have an idea what it does.'

'I couldn't find any match on the database,' Ianto said. *'Nothing even close.'*

Toshiko pulled her glasses off and turned them around thoughtfully. She held up the strange little device. 'These could be magnifying glasses of some kind.' She looked through one. 'That's strange. I can't see anything but darkness.' She put it down again. 'Look. The glass appears clear here. Pale yellow just like the light around it. But if you look through it –' she handed it to Ianto – 'there's nothing but darkness.'

'She's right,' Ianto said, peering through it. 'Strange.'

'Well, it's a quiet night. Have a play with it. I'll be in the office doing all the accounts that Jack's avoided for the past three months.'

It was two hours later that Toshiko called her back down to the lab. For a moment, she didn't say anything but just stared at the large box on the table.

'Is that what I think it is?'

'Sorry, yes.' Toshiko pushed her glasses back up her nose. 'I didn't want to disturb you until I knew whether it would work, so I just got it out of the vault myself.'

'I'm surprised you could find it.' The container that now held the small metal credit card looked just like a Perspex box. It wasn't, of course. Perspex could never do what this could.

'It did take a while. Our system for filing this stuff could do with updating. Anyway, I just

thought that given the density of the metal for an item so small, perhaps it needed a pressure far greater than we could apply to activate it.'

'Go on.' Suzie folded her arms. Toshiko might be something of a mouse – and to be fair had become twice as irritating since she'd started mooning around Owen like a wet blanket – but she was clever. Which was good because since she'd been adding quite heavily to her extracurricular activities, Suzie's own brain was invariably operating at half-speed when at work.

'Well, I was right. At least halfway. Watch.'

Taped to the inside of the clear box was a small explosive charge. Small in terms of size at least. Suzie had seen one of those go off and take half a house down. She took a step back out of habit rather than necessity as Toshiko clicked the remote detonator in her hand. The silent explosion filled the box with a bright, white light and Suzie squinted against it, turning away slightly.

'Now look,' Toshiko said.

The credit card sat undamaged, but slightly changed, in the centre of the alien container. The three clear stones that were embedded in it had changed colour. The one in the centre flashed red, and the other two had turned an almost milky matt black.

'So you've turned it on...' Suzie leaned forward to get a closer look. 'But what does it do?'

'I'm monitoring the particles and energy in there. It draws energy in to kick-start itself, but then a different energy is being emitted. Nothing

that the system recognises, but something is coming through there. Something quite powerful. I think it might be some kind of alien remote viewer. I don't think it's a weapon at any rate. Whatever it is, it could be a great source of energy if we could just figure it out.'

The red centre light dimmed. 'What's it doing?'

'Turning itself off. That's happened twice now. Maybe it needs a renewable energy supply on this side to keep working.'

'Or maybe whoever's looking through it didn't see anything that interested them.'

She smiled at Tosh. 'Good work. Put it in the vault for now. I can't see any immediate use for it.'

'Will do.'

'And don't forget to log it on the system! Let's get these files workable.'

Suzie left it two days before taking the item back out of the vault. If Jack had been interested he would have wanted to see it by now, but he hadn't given it a mention. The device was already forgotten, just one more piece of Rift junk washed up in Cardiff, now safely stored away. She slipped it into her pocket. It created energy, that's what Toshiko had said. Perhaps if she could harness that energy it could enhance the power of the Resurrection glove?

Chapter Four

'Blimey,' Andy said.

Cutler thought his sergeant's reaction was somewhat understated, but then newly promoted Andy Davidson wasn't much of a swearer. His own internal reaction had featured much stronger terms, like those being muttered by the Scene of Crime boys as they arrived.

'It goes without saying no details of this hit the press,' he said, letting them pass. 'I don't want to hear that you've even mentioned it to your girlfriends, wives or mothers, all right?'

'Who'd tell their mother about this?' Andy asked. He had a point.

The woman sat against the wall, her legs straight out in front of her and slightly apart. She was small and petite and, even though she had to be in her fifties, the pose made her look like a doll. A badly damaged doll admittedly, given how her eyes appeared to be missing from their sockets. Blood had run in two thick streams down her cheeks and onto her shirt and her mouth was slightly open.

'It's like something out of one of those Japanese horror films,' Andy muttered.

Cutler, careful not to touch anything even though he had gloves and plastic slippers on, crouched by the dead woman.

'So, Doc,' he said to the figure mirroring his position, 'what have we got?'

'Hard to tell at the moment.' Dr Spanton's Birmingham accent was as out of place as Cutler's own North London mumble amidst all the gentle Welsh lilt. The doctor hadn't been in Cardiff that long. Transferred down for a quiet life. He wasn't getting one today.

Cutler looked at the dead woman. 'You seen anything like this before?'

'Nope.' Dr Spanton leaned closer to the body, his plastic suit rustling. 'And I think I'd be happy not to see anything like it again.' He lifted the woman's blouse. 'There's a nasty stab wound here. Straight into the liver I would say – I'll let you know for certain when she's on the slab – but it should be the injury that killed her.'

'Should be?' Cutler frowned.

'I'm surprised by the lack of blood. There's so much from her eyes and so little from here. It should have been pumping out of her, but there's nothing.'

'Post-mortem wound?'

'Even if it was, unless the killer hung around for a while before delivering it, there should still be more blood. A conundrum.'

'So what about the eyes?' Cutler asked. 'Are

they gouged out? Cut out?'

'I wish. Look.' Spanton pointed at something shining in the mess of the woman's smart blouse. 'That looks like vitreous gel to me. It's the substance inside the back of the eye. There's a lot of it.' He looked up. 'She's wearing what's left of her eyes in all this blood. It's impossible but it's almost as if they exploded.'

'Sir?' called Andy.

Cutler nodded at Dr Spanton and left him to get on with his unpleasant job. 'What have you got?'

'Her name's Janet Scott,' Andy told him. 'She's 54, divorced. Worked here since the place opened twelve years ago.'

'Sir?' A disembodied voice called out from somewhere beyond Andy. 'CCTV's been disabled. Nothing on the computer.'

Cutler sighed. Nothing was ever easy. So they'd learned the killer wasn't stupid. 'What else?' He returned his attention to Andy.

'About Janet Scott? Not much. She was working on her own today, but that wasn't normal. Her colleague had called in sick.'

'One person working alone in a safety deposit company? Seems a bit odd.'

'It's not the smartest area of town. And this isn't a bank.' Andy shrugged. 'I doubt these boxes are filled with diamonds. Plus, there's no record of any thefts or break-ins at the premises, so I guess she felt quite relaxed.'

'That was a mistake,' Cutler said, glancing

back at the body. 'Who found her?'

'The colleague. A Mr John Askew. He's the owner, actually. Rang to check on her and after getting no answer several times came down here. Called 999 straight away. His wife verifies his story.'

'Make sure he doesn't call anyone else. I don't want too many details in the press just yet.'

'Not a serial, is it?'

'It's unpleasant. That's enough.' Cutler couldn't shake the unease. It wasn't just the murder. Gruesome as this one was, he'd seen worse. There was just something about it that made him think he wasn't seeing the bigger picture. That this should be ringing alarm bells for him about something just out of his mental reach.

'Can we find out who was the last client in?'

'I'm ahead of you, sir. Mr Askew checked before we got here, even though he was shocked. PC Weir double-checked the system and got the same answer.'

'Which is?' Andy Davidson had only been on attachment with him for a couple of weeks, but Cutler had already discovered how hard it was to get him to the point.

'A woman named Eryn Bunting accessed her deposit box at 11.45 this morning. The box itself is still in that private room.' He nodded over at one of the doors behind the slumped body of Janet Scott. 'That's where clients do whatever they need to do before returning it.'

'I presume the box is empty.'

'Correct.'

'Who is she?'

'Her address was on the records and we've got someone over there checking it out. This was only her second visit. She was here in 2007 to open her account and that was it until today.'

'I doubt very much that whoever we're looking for is the person at that address. Like you said. This isn't a bank. From my experience the people who have safety deposit boxes have something to hide. They're unlikely to give their own name and address, and it's unlikely, as long as the annual fees are paid, that anyone checks too thoroughly. Wouldn't be good for business.'

He looked around him. Suddenly confined space felt oppressive. 'Let's get out of here and get a coffee. There's nothing we can do until we get some more information.'

Twenty minutes later, the two men were sitting in a basement bar around the corner when Andy Davidson's phone began to ring. Cutler was sipping a large, frothing cappuccino, but the slim, fair-haired sergeant had opted for a lemonade. Cutler had almost smiled. Who ordered lemonade these days? He watched as Andy sipped it and was about to smile and make a joke about what had policing come to and why weren't they drinking beer in a pub, when he froze. As he blinked, Andy Davidson disappeared. In his place was a tall man in his late thirties. His hair was dark, unlike Andy's. He was handsome, but he wasn't smiling.

The weight of the world sat on his shoulders.

Cutler's breath raced in his ears, drowning him in the sound. The man was sitting on the stool next to Cutler and sipping a glass of water. He turned to look at Cutler, his mouth moving but in the roar that filled his head, Cutler couldn't hear the words. He frowned, his own mouth moving. This was wrong. This was very wrong. He blinked again, but the man was still there. What was his brain doing? Had he been drugged? Was this LSD at work? The man was still speaking to him, and he reached forward and gripped Cutler's arm.

'Sir?'

The word cut through the white noise in his head, distant at first, and then suddenly loud.

'Sir?' Andy repeated.

The man was gone. The sergeant was back, his lemonade – *just like a glass of water* – sitting on the bar. Cutler looked down. Andy's hand was on his arm. His other held his mobile phone.

'Are you OK, sir?'

'Yes,' he said, his breath catching slightly in his throat. 'Yes, sorry. Just wandered off somewhere for a moment.'

'You looked like you'd seen a ghost.' Andy frowned, concerned. 'Maybe time to lay off the caffeine.'

'Maybe.' Cutler smiled. He took a deep breath. It had been nothing. Just his brain playing a trick on him. Maybe Andy was right. Maybe he did drink too much coffee.

'That was Jon Weir calling, sir,' Andy said.

'They've checked out the owner of that box, and you were right. Eryn Bunting is a schoolteacher. Knows nothing about any safety deposit box and has been teaching all day. She was in a lesson when Janet Scott was killed.'

'Get back on the phone. I want a list of her friends and neighbours. Anyone she shares any rubbish bins with. Someone used her ID. She must know our killer.' Cutler looked at the half-drunk coffee. He suddenly didn't want it any more. 'Sod it,' he said. 'Let's go and take a look ourselves. I could use some fresh air.'

He was glad to get out of the bar and back out onto the streets. He wanted to put some distance between himself and that strange moment. It was just his brain, he thought again, playing tricks on him. Happened to everyone. He climbed into the passenger seat and stared out of the window as Andy drove.

It was the coat that was bothering him. Why would his brain have dressed up a figment of his imagination in a Second World War greatcoat?

Chapter Five

It was amazing what the internet could do when you knew how, and Suzie had made sure she'd known how. Within three hours spent hunched over the slim laptop, she'd created a passable history for Sue Costa, her new persona. A few brief news stories on the right websites, the inevitable Linkedin account, and the activation of a website for the fictional company that she had apparently just left the employment of.

It would be enough should anyone conduct a quick search on her. She doubted they would. Most people were relatively slack, and the higher up the food chain you went the more likely it was that you'd presume someone else had already done the checking. She remote accessed the required email account and smiled to find that it was still working. She'd been prepared to run a dictionary attack to find a new password, but it seemed that even in the Department no one in the admin offices listened to the drill of 'change your passwords frequently'. She sent her message and then logged out. Everything was ready.

She poured herself a drink and then paced the bland, overly modern flat, before eventually stopping by the window and looking out over the water that glinted in the moonlight. She knew she should run. Get out of the country. Go and live in some warmer climate and sit by a pool all day. That was probably the sensible thing to do, but she needed to know exactly what the situation was first. And anyway, she felt like being a little daring.

She smiled and let a mouthful of brandy burn her mouth before she swallowed it. It made her feel alive again. She would go abroad soon enough, but not to laze around in the sunshine. Maybe she'd set up a business of her own. Her eyes hardened. She could turn a hobby to a profit. Everybody wanted someone else dead, and she was more than happy to make them that way.

The sea was black and endless beneath the night sky. From behind the closed sliding door, it was also silent. There was no gentle splashing of waves as they rolled over each other to spill in surf upon the stony beach. Suzie stared, and to her there was no nature in that eternity of darkness. She shivered. It was like death out there, waiting to reclaim her. Her eyes were tired from the hours spent concentrating on the small computer screen, but she didn't want to sleep. She had a horrible feeling it would try to take her while she slept. She didn't like her fear. She *was* death. She had nothing to fear from that darkness.

She wondered about perhaps drinking some

more until she finally passed out, but instead of walking to the kitchen, she found that she'd headed to the hall and was pulling on a coat. Her heart thumped and she smiled as the terrible dimension behind her eyes cooled her insides. The surprise she'd felt at its presence was fading and, as it looked out through her, she turned inwards to explore it. She gasped. This wasn't the nothingness of death. This was no empty, black non-existence. This was... she couldn't find the words for the sudden dread and terror she felt. *Evil? Was that it?* It was as close as she could come.

She pulled back and took a moment to compose herself. Whatever it was, it had brought her back to life.

She smiled as she passed the mirror in the hallway. Her eyes swirled slightly and she caught a glimpse of what others would see. A glimpse of the horror of that strange dimension. Her eyes were a gateway and she was death. Energy pulsed inside her. It was *hungry*. If she fed it some more, then perhaps she wouldn't need to sleep at all. Her heart raced and she gripped the knife. The excitement she felt had nothing to do with the need to feed the beast within, and everything with her own desire to kill. The front door clicked shut behind her and she rode the quiet lift down to street level. She was smiling when she stepped out into the night streets, and wondered, idly, when murder had turned from a practical necessity, to something she enjoyed so much?

*

Detective Inspector Tom Cutler couldn't sleep. Something was bothering him. Lots of things were bothering him, in fact. It wasn't just the man in the long greatcoat that he had seen in that weird moment in the bar. That did keep itching at his head – especially the coat – but it was more than that. That was like a side show to the main event and he couldn't figure out why. It was something to do with the poor dead woman. Something to do with her eyes filled him with a quiet dread. The greatcoat. The eyes. There was something there that he just couldn't connect; or something that his brain was refusing to connect.

As his brain whirred, he'd given up any attempt at sleep at around 1 a.m. He'd got out of bed, made a cup of tea, and then turned the TV on. There was bound to be some sport showing somewhere on the millions of channels he had and, unlike most men, if there was one thing that was likely to cure his insomnia, it was watching sport. He'd found some baseball and tried to zone out in front of it. He sipped his tea. He'd forgotten sugar.

In the kitchen he pulled open a drawer for a teaspoon and then just stared at it. His brain quietened. Something just out of reach played in his mind, emptying everything else out. He closed the drawer, opened it, and then closed it again. His tea sat cooling on the side as he worked his way around the small room, pulling open cupboards and then closing them, repeating the action several times with each before moving on to the next. He worked on autopilot. A film settled on his tea. On the TV one or other of the teams won the game, and the commentators moved onto something new. At some point Cutler sat down.

He woke up with a stiff neck at 5 a.m. to the sound of rugby playing out somewhere in the world. He stared at the TV confused. His head was thumping, his throat was sore and his mouth tasted like shit. He frowned. It wasn't shit. It was...

There was a mug of tea on the low coffee table in front of him and something was floating on its surface. He leaned forward. It couldn't be. What had he done? He stared at the cigarette butts floating in the cold liquid. After a moment he counted them up. Six? He'd smoked six cigarettes in the night? He frowned and rubbed his head. He needed painkillers, that was for sure. He remembered not being able to sleep and getting up and making a drink. That was about it. Had he hit the bottle at some point? Surely he'd remember *something*?

He shuffled into the kitchen. Pills, and then back to bed for a couple of hours. Maybe he'd remember more then. His hand paused as he reached for the handle. Brown masking tape ran in three strips across the two doors keeping them shut. Confused, he looked around him. All the cupboard doors had been taped shut. And the drawers. His headache momentarily forgotten, he walked slowly around his flat, his heart thumping steadily more loudly with each step. It wasn't just the kitchen. All the cupboards and doors were taped shut.

What the hell had he been doing all night?
What the hell was going on?

Chapter Six

'Let me get this straight.' The doctor was sweating slightly. 'You want me to cut you open and sew this into the back of your skin?' He held up the sealed object.

'Yes,' Suzie smiled at him. 'I thought I'd made that perfectly clear. It's not difficult to understand.'

'Do you know how dangerous that could be?'

It was late at night and Suzie didn't have time for games. So much time was wasted spelling out the obvious, and she had to be back at the Hub by 9 a.m. She wanted this in and tested by then.

'I think I probably know that better than you.' She lay down on the table in his surgery. 'People have metal placed in their bodies all the time. Pacemakers. Steel pins. Just think of this as something like that.'

'But what does it do?' Under the white light, his balding head was sweating. He really was an unpleasant little man.

'I'm not entirely sure.' She was running out of patience, especially given that in a couple of hours all his questions would be irrelevant anyway. 'But that's my concern, not yours.' Her dark eyes sparkled with good-humour. 'What you need to weigh up is this. You either do what I ask, or I'll be reporting you for that stash of unpleasant and definitely illegal pornography you have. You AND your little group of like-minded friends. Do what I say, and you can carry on with your sick pleasures. Seems like a no-brainer to me.'

She smiled as he started to prep the room. 'Oh,' she added. 'Local anaesthetic only, please. And don't get any ridiculous ideas about killing me on the table. That happens, your secrets definitely come out.'

She killed him as soon as she could comfortably move. He wasn't expecting it, but she saw the abject disbelief in his eyes as they widened in the moment just before she pulled the knife out of her boot and stabbed him with it.

'Sorry, Doc,' she whispered. 'Needs must.'

He crumpled to the floor in an unpleasantly pudgy heap, blood pooling underneath him. She checked he had no pulse and then, ignoring the pain in her stomach that was creeping past the painkillers, she pulled the Resurrection gauntlet out of her holdall. She smiled. If this thing inside her could pump out energy, then maybe it could extend the effects of the glove when she and it were connected. There was only one way to find out. She pulled it on, activated it, and then lifted the man's head.

His eyes flew open; the usual mix of confusion and fear.

'I thought I was dead... I thought I was... you stabbed me... you...'

'Shhhhh.' Suzie cut him off. 'You ARE dead. Well, not right in this minute. And I mean literally this minute, but you are dead.'

'I don't understand... I don't... Oh god, there was nothing. Nothing.'

Suzie ignored his panicked mutterings and counted down the seconds on her watch. It didn't feel any different. If the thing inside her was doing anything, she didn't know about it.

'Please help me...' Tears filled the doctor's eyes. 'Please... I've got a family...'

'Children?' Suzie asked. She couldn't keep the disdain from her voice. Even if the device extended the power of the gauntlet, she would kill this man again. He disgusted her. She might be a murderer, but she wasn't a monster like he was.

As it was, she didn't have to. His minute and a half of extra time played out and his eyes shut. He was gone. She'd hoped for longer.

'Shit.' She took the glove off and then washed the knife. That was disappointing. She peered down at the bandaging over her slim stomach. As plans went, she hadn't entirely thought that one through. And she was normally so bloody organised. In her haste to see if the device could somehow enhance the energy of the glove, she'd not thought beyond getting it inside her and then testing it on the doctor. She hadn't considered how she was going

to get it out again.

She sighed, and gathered her things together. Oh well, she thought. It could stay there for now. It wasn't as if it was doing her any harm. It would take a building falling down around her to get it to start working if Toshiko's experiments were anything to go by. She didn't think that would be happening any time soon.

Chapter Seven

The only time that Rebecca Devlin ever really longed for the old single days – or even the days before the kids came along – was first thing in the morning. She wasn't designed for all the rushing around. She was a cup of tea in bed and wake up slowly to the news kind of girl.

She caught sight of her reflection in the oven glass. She wasn't much of a 'girl' any more, not wrapped as she was in her fluffy dressing gown over her tatty pyjamas, and with her hair yanked back in a scrunchie that was clearly too young for her 39 going on 50 tired skin. It wasn't the sexiest of looks, but who the hell had time to be sexy with three kids and a husband? Sex was a luxury, and luxuries were for when half-terms rolled around, or she and Gary managed to sneak a few days away to themselves. The rest of the time – as it had been for the past month or so – sex was just one more thing on a very long 'to do' list. Long gone were the days of ripping each other's clothes off on the stairs or the sofa, or in fact, she thought as she put the cereal boxes down, right here on this table.

With a pan on to boil – her life would be so much easier if her mother hadn't instilled the virtues of a proper breakfast into her – she took the eggs from the fridge and popped them in the water, before putting the carton in the bin. Or at least trying to.

'Bloody hell, Gary,' she muttered. The bin was pretty much overflowing. He'd said he'd change it before he went to bed after the game had finished. He'd *promised* her. She could hear herself nagging at him as she'd gone up the stairs, dog-tired at about half-nine. She knew he hated changing the bins (although maybe if just once he did it before it was overflowing and likely to spill all over the kitchen floor then it would be a less unpleasant job), but she hated changing the bed sheets, and she still did it. She didn't ask him to do much, and he still didn't do it. Just once she'd like to change places. She'd go off and sit behind a desk all day and he could manage the house and kids.

A black and white cat wound itself around her legs as she carefully pulled the black sack free and tied it closed. It sat by an empty bowl decorated with fish, and then meowed.

'In a minute, Sailor.' She grabbed the bag and headed for the front door, trying to fight her rising irritation. It was a two-minute job and it really didn't matter, but somehow it did, because it was *his* job and by not doing it, he made her feel like *she* didn't matter. She also knew that if she said anything, it would just sound like nagging, and sometimes she didn't like how she sounded exactly like her mother when she heard herself. Still, she thought, as she reflected on her parents and how much her mother had done around the house compared to her father, maybe her mother had had a point.

'Breakfast in ten!' she called upstairs. Not that anyone would hear with all the radios and music coming from each bedroom.

It was still early and the street outside was relatively quiet as she added the black sack to the main bin and wheeled it to the pavement to join the others waiting for collection. Heels clicked on the pavement ahead and she looked up to see a striking-looking woman walking past. There was a cat-like elegance in her long slim limbs and clear features, and she walked with confidence.

She's about my age, Rebecca thought in dismay, as she caught the woman's brown eyes and smiled awkwardly. The same age and yet so different. Once again, her dowdiness overwhelmed her. She needed to take it in hand, she decided, looking at the other woman's sleek black trousers and patent boots. She wasn't old. She needed to stop acting it.

The woman gave her a brief smile in return and then passed by. Rebecca watched her go. The early morning sunshine was bright and the woman cast a long shadow behind her. Rebecca frowned. Too long. She tilted her head slightly. It was too long and too dark, and looked as if it was stretching backwards trying to reach her. With the curiosity of a child, Rebecca stuck her foot out, letting her slipper catch the edge of it. She smiled slightly. It was just a shadow. The woman's heels faded and eventually the strip of darkness moved from Rebecca Devlin's front door. She watched it go.

Back in the kitchen she checked the water was starting to bubble and then took a fresh bin bag from under the sink. She stared out of the window, caught for a moment in the glare of light. Her head ached. The bubbling and the music from upstairs faded and her heart thumped. What was wrong? What was wrong with her? She looked down at the bag in her hands and shook it out, desperately trying to shake away the sudden fear in the pit of her stomach.

The bag opened up and all she could see was darkness. She thought of the heels tapping along the pavement. She thought of the strange shadow. Images flashed behind her eyes. She gasped.

Red shoes. Running. Heels. Hers. She hasn't worn shoes like that in a long time, and wishing that she hadn't tonight. She thinks maybe she should kick them off and go barefoot, but the street is filthy and she's scared that the seconds it takes will be enough for her to lose this race. She's losing it anyway, she knows that. It's right behind her. She keeps running, heels or no heels, putting her faith in the red patent Kurt Geigers that she loves to not let her break her ankle. These were her favourite shoes, her date shoes from years gone by, and as she's running in them she's wondering how such a good night could be turning out so badly.

She wants to laugh. She wants to cry. She really, really doesn't want to die.

Her hair flies out behind her, and she can barely breathe. She hasn't run like this since school and that was too many years ago now. Why did she go out with the girls? Why did she listen to Gary that it was a good idea for her to let her hair down? It wasn't seeming like such a good bloody idea now.

The thing growls and she can almost feel its hot breath. It had been her taxi driver. Her stupid taxi driver. She'd got in, still laughing, waved goodbye to Gillian and Kate, and given him her address. Her feet had ached then. If she got out of this alive then they were going to need a good long soak. She giggled again.

Thank God she'd got out when he changed. When he turned round and she saw his awful burning face and he'd reached for her. Please God, she thought, as she pushed herself to get around the corner up ahead, please God let me get out of this alive. Please God, I don't want to die, please God, and what the hell is it anyway –

She rounds the corner and collides with someone's chest.

'Getoutofmyway! Getoutofmyway!' she screams as panic takes over. It's coming, it's coming and if she doesn't keep running…

'It's OK.' Arms wrap round her. 'Owen, what are you doing?'

'Sorry. My eye's not in on this thing yet.' A sound rushes past her. Air. Movement. Then a howl of rage.

'That's better. Got him now.'

A female laugh. 'If your aim is that bad no wonder the toilet in the Hub is always such a mess.'

'Save the jokes, Tosh. They don't suit you.' A pause. 'What the hell is it anyway? Not seen one like that before.'

Her heart thumps as the voices, and two sets of footsteps, move past. She keeps her head buried in the chest of the man whose arms have stayed wrapped around her.

'Just get it contained and in the SUV.' His chest vibrates when he speaks and she finds it comforting. She's going to live. She's alive. She starts to cry all over again.

'Yes, boss.'

When he finally pulls back, he's smiling. Blue eyes, dark hair and a grin that could set Hollywood alight. 'You're safe now,' he says.

'Who are you?' she mumbles, aware that her mascara has no doubt run down her face and that she's soaked in sweat. Not a good look for a woman past 30. She wonders why how she looks suddenly matters when barely five minutes ago she was just desperate to stay alive.

'I'm Captain Jack Harkness,' the man says, and she loves the American lilt in his voice. 'That's Owen Harper, and the lovely lady carrying the box is Toshiko Sato.' Rebecca watches as the man and woman nod and smile at her as they head to the rear of their large black car.

'But who are you?' she asks again, as her

heartbeat slows to somewhere near normal. 'And what was that... thing?'

'Us? We're Torchwood.' He grins. 'Now come and tell me exactly what happened. Then we'll make you a nice cup of tea and get you home.'

Torchwood. She stared into the black bag. A void of emptiness. The tea. They'd made her tea, and it made her forget everything. Been chased by muggers, that's what she told Gary when she got home. She'd laughed it off. It had all been vague. Muggers. She was sure. She'd been chased by something anyway. Gary had been surprised at how quickly she'd got over the ordeal. So had she, but it had simply slipped from her memory over a few days. Become like a dream.

Torchwood.

She thought of the woman outside. The shadow in her wake. Her heart thumped. The shadow was Torchwood business. Where were they? Gone. She knew it. Who would save them all when the shadows grew longer? When *that place* came? She gasped, her hands flying to her mouth as she caught a glimpse of what would come to pass. She thought of the American in the greatcoat. Captain Jack. *You're safe now*. That's what he had said. She wasn't safe. Not at all.

Behind her the pan was boiling over, steam rising in the small room. She didn't notice. Her mind was lost in what she knew of the shadows. Her foot had touched it. Now, with her mind and memory unlocked it was as if she could truly *see* it. The awfulness inside. The pain that waited.

The horror that lived there. It was coming. *The screaming of millions.*

She took the black marker pen from the scribble board on the wall that told her on Friday she and the boys had dentist appointments, Saturday was football for Noah, and where a shopping voucher was attached by a magnet they bought in Cornwall last year. She rubbed it all out with her dressing-gown sleeve. It didn't matter. None of it mattered. Her mind was a fog of darkness and she scrawled her message in big black letters.

I REMEMBER

It was all she could say. It was the remembering that had done it. The handsome American with his cup of tea, *here you go, drink that, it'll make you feel better,* had made her forget, but now that the remembering was done, she could see what was coming. *Did he know that would happen when he messed with her brain, the handsome American, and oh no her mascara has run and he's so breathtakingly handsome and who are you anyway?*

Torchwood.

She pulled a knife from the block. Her mind was lost in the darkness. She wouldn't let it come for her. She couldn't. Not the screaming. Not her screaming. Upstairs, a million miles away, the music was turned off and a door opened. She plunged the knife deep into her stomach.

There was screaming when she died. She could hear it as she stared up at the white ceiling that needed a fresh coat of paint. But it was OK, she thought, a small smile drifting across her lips. It was only her children screaming. That was fine. It was only her children. Not her soul.

Chapter Eight

'We're not getting much on Eryn Bunting or any of her neighbours,' Andy Davidson said. 'She's lived in the same house since 2005, and her boyfriend moved in in 2006. She's never been burgled or had any other crime perpetrated on the property. None of the neighbours have any criminal records – apart from one man, several doors down, but that was a drunk-driving conviction.'

'Maybe it was just opportunistic then,' Cutler mused, leaning back on the desk. He'd slept like a log for the two hours between five and seven and felt surprisingly awake. His mouth still had the lingering taste of cigarettes though, despite having brushed his teeth twice. It was the only solid reminder he had that anything strange had happened in the night. He put it down to alcohol. Or maybe sleep-walking of some kind, not that he'd done that before, but there was always a first time. Whatever it was, he'd put it out of his head. Apart from the cigarettes. Looking at the crime scene photos on the board, the before and after images of poor Janet Scott in particular, wasn't helping.

'Unlikely. Eryn Bunting keeps all her bank statements and payslips.' Andy sipped his tea. 'I didn't actually know people like that existed. I don't know where my payslip is for last month, let alone last year, and the last thing I want to keep in my flat is evidence of my overdraft, but Eryn Bunting is a filer. At least she was until everything went online.' He smiled. 'She's a paper-saver too. But she had her bank slips for 2007. There was one missing.'

'Really?' Cutler frowned. Thus far, his money had been on the killer just having gone through a random recycling bag until he found something. 'Is she in a flat or a house? Any way our killer might have been able to steal her post?'

'Again unlikely. And anyway, if she was this anal about filing, she'd have noticed if a statement didn't turn up.'

'Anything on Janet Scott?'

'Clean as a whistle.'

'Great.' Cutler chewed the end of a pen. 'Well, until forensics get back to us, we've got nothing. Let's hope we get something from the body. The killer must have left something behind. Hair or clothes fibre.'

'Yeah, but how long will that take to come back?'

'Fast I hope. We're not exactly overrun with this kind of murder. We should get bumped to the top of the list.'

'Sir?' A uniformed constable, Sue Fellowes, interrupted them from the doorway. 'Have you got a minute? Could you come and have a look at something for us?'

Cutler smiled slightly. If anything odd came into the station then they always got him to take a look at it first, as if just because he'd been a DI in London for several years that meant he must have seen anything and everything.

'Sure,' he said. 'What is it?'

'Come and see.'

'We just weren't sure,' Fellowes said. 'Is it from that site? The head bit's not there, though. And I don't know what these things look like really. I haven't paid much attention to them when I've been down the Bay.'

Cutler stared at the contamination suit laid out on the table. 'Where did you say this was found?'

'It was stuffed behind some bins at the back of a restaurant. The chef found it this morning.'

'And no helmet?'

She shook her head. 'Is that important? You think it's from the army site then?'

Cutler didn't answer, his memory replaying a scene from the previous morning. A suited figure striding casually out of the site, suit still on. Why hadn't he stopped them or said something? It seemed crazy looking back on it. He was a policeman. He should have *known* there was something odd about that. It was as if he somehow zoned out when he was staring at the people working behind the barricades. A sudden flash of memory hit him. Taping up the cupboards. A terrible sense of something being opened that shouldn't be. He pushed it away.

'It looks like it,' he said.

'Shall I call them and see if there's one missing?'

'No,' Cutler said quickly. 'I'll take it back. If this is theirs then someone's broken their protocols. If you call it through, they'll all know. I'll go and see that Commander Jackson.' His voice was steady but his heart was thumping. He was going to get behind the barricades. 'You can get on to the council and check how often the public waste bins in the bay are emptied. If they haven't been done since yesterday morning, get down there and see if you can find the helmet in one of them.'

'Yes, sir.'

He was almost at the site when his phone starting ringing and he very nearly didn't answer it. What was it about this place that fired him up so much? It was like it made the rest of the world entirely unimportant. As if there was something here that his brain needed to concentrate on to the detriment of everything else.

His phone didn't shut up, and he finally took the call. It was his sergeant.

'What's up, Andy? Forensics can't be back already, surely?'

'No.' Davidson sounded strange. Subdued. 'No, they're not, but they're going to have their hands full from now on.'

'What are you on about?' As he approached the

barrier an army guard took a few steps towards him. Cutler stopped and put the black sack containing the suit on the ground and rummaged in his jacket for his police ID.

'Three more bodies have been found.'

Cutler's hand paused. 'What?'

'Exactly like Janet Scott. Stabbed to death, and with the eyes – well – whatever happened to hers, its happened to these three.'

'Shit.' Cutler flashed his badge at the waiting soldier. 'I'll drop this off and be right back. I take it the scenes are secured?'

'Yes. But the victims were all found in public places. The press have already been on wanting something from us and local news are running it on the TV. The DCI wants you back here as soon as.'

'I will be. Give me ten minutes.' He ended the call before Andy could say any more. He didn't want to say outright that he was going into the site. The DCI wouldn't be happy about that. He'd expect him just to hand the suit over and turn around. That's exactly what Cutler would pretend he'd done when he got back, but it wasn't what he was going to do. Five minutes – that was all he needed. He just wanted to get behind that barrier. He couldn't help himself.

He'd called ahead and once the soldier had passed a wary eye over his ID and peered into the bin bag Cutler was carrying, he led him behind the barrier. The DI wondered why his mouth suddenly dried. It wasn't as if he could see much more than he had from the other side. The excavation of the site itself was still hidden by huge walls of white tarpaulin and it was a calm day so the entrance wasn't even flapping slightly in the wind. His brain itched as if ants were scurrying over his synapses trying to fire them up to something. He blinked and saw the flash of a greatcoat and a charming smile. What was it about this place that bothered and fascinated him so much?

He followed the soldier up the steps of the Portakabin and waited to be allowed in.

Chapter Nine

Andrew Murray had smiled at the woman as he got into the lift and she got out. He hadn't noticed her here before and he was sure he would have done. She was beautiful. Maybe she'd just moved in. He hadn't seen any removal vans, though, and, as he worked nights and suffered from pretty bad insomnia, he normally had a pretty good idea of who came and went from the block. The ability to stand out on his balcony and see what was happening in the world was one of the advantages of having a flat higher up in the building. He found it quite mesmerising watching the daily traffic. When the weather was good, he would people watch for hours. It allowed his mainly sleep-deprived brain to switch off a little.

It was nice to know that at least some people out there were having a life. A combination of an essentially bland personality, combined with a liking for all the wrong kinds of foods had led to a relatively lonely life for Andrew. Not that he overly minded, but there were times when, especially after a quiet shift at work managing the small supermarket, and when sleep totally evaded him, that he wished he had larger social life than the occasional drink with colleagues or other branch managers, and the inevitable weekly visit to his ageing parents for a Sunday roast which was mainly spent avoiding the question of why he wasn't married yet.

His mother seemed completely baffled by his single status, as if her balding son was Cardiff's answer to Brad Pitt and there should be a queue of women wanting to breed with him. As it was, he'd never been overly concerned with the thought of a wife, and he definitely didn't want children. Most of the time he was perfectly content with the sex that the internet and various chat rooms had to offer him. Life was much simpler that way. But he still enjoyed spending time watching others, who had more inclination to grab life by the horns, as they dashed around.

He and the tall, slim woman stepped around each other. He'd been so lost in his own sleepless thoughts that he'd almost walked right into her as the lift doors opened, and they'd smiled at each other as strangers do in those awkward moments when their personal space has been invaded. She smelled great. He was close enough to know that. Expensive perfume. Nothing cheap. *Coco*? The name came to him in an instant. How the hell did he know that?

Her smiled dropped as his sudden confusion stopped him from shifting sideways to let her pass and he felt a shiver of something. It was almost recognition. He must have seen her in the building before, after all. He frowned slightly. Strange he didn't remember her. He muttered an apology and stepped to one side as she pushed past him. His delay had made her drop her pretence at politeness and she flashed him an irritated glare. A chill crept up his toes and he looked down. He was standing in her shadow. Within minutes, both she and her shadow had gone, but he remained where he was, staring at the ground.

'What the hell is that? It stinks?' It's the doctor speaking. Owen? Is that his name? Andrew stands shivering in the street, still soaked from head to foot in whatever the substance is that has come out of that thing that he'd thought was Alison. He is NEVER going on a date again.

'This slime smells better than that.' The dark-haired doctor peers into his face. 'Don't worry. You're going to be OK,' he says.

'Coco by Chanel.' The young Japanese woman looks up from where she's crouched by the mess, and smiles. Andrew watches her and doesn't know if he's more terrified of how calm these three are than he was of Alison, whose skin peeled off as she came for him. Who are they? They're acting as if this sort of thing happens every day.

'Good call, Tosh!' The third person, a beautiful dark-haired woman, smiles. She's leaning forward and putting lipstick on, using the wing mirror of the black SUV. 'Timelessly classy.'

'What? Like you?' the doctor mutters. The woman comes over and peers at Andrew, and he

catches the scent of her perfume. He thinks he might be sick. Alison had been wearing perfume. Cheaper than this one. Stronger. Why would a thing wear perfume? He thinks he might cry. None of this makes any sense.

'Yes, like me. I hope there's none of this stuff on my shoes.' She checks her heels. Andrew stares. He's shaking all over. When he looks at her, all he sees is Alison. Just before her skin... her skin... He can't even think it. Were all women like that? How would he be able to tell?

'You two can finish up here, right? If I miss this engagement party, I'll never be forgiven. I'll grab a taxi.'

Engagement party? How can she be thinking of going to a party? Now? After this?

'No problem,' Tosh says. The doctor scrapes gunk from a patch of Andrew's cheek and puts it in a sample jar. 'Yeah, have fun. Think of us doing the paperwork.'

'See you in the morning.' The woman tosses a smile over her shoulder as her heels click away towards the main streets.

The doctor fetches him a towel from the SUV, and Andrew stands shivering and shaking while Tosh whistles as she carefully picks up Alison's skin – Alison's skin, that's Alison's skin – and puts it into a container.

'We'll have to hose the street down,' she says. 'This stuff has got everywhere.'

'You can manage that.'

'You're the one that shot her,' Tosh says as

she hands Andrew the towel. 'My vote was for containing it.'

'It was going to eat him. The skin was already off.' The doctor, Owen, takes the container and puts it into the back of the van. 'Shooting was the best option.'

'You're always so quick to shoot,' Tosh says. 'We had time.' She looks at Andrew who is just standing still, the towel in one hand. 'It's all right. She's gone. You were luckier than the two men she went out with earlier this week. Now wipe that stuff off you, and we'll get you home.'

Owen hands Andrew a small glass of what looks like brandy. A drink of some sort, anyway. 'Drink that. There's something in it that will make you feel better. Trust me.'

'Who are you?' he gets the question out eventually, his voice trembling as much as the rest of his body. 'Who are you?'

'Us?' Tosh says, and both she and Owen smile. 'We're Torchwood.'

Andrew drinks.

Torchwood.

He remembered. His legs felt unsteady with the sudden unlocked information. Alison. The thing she became. He couldn't remember getting back to his flat, but instead just found himself standing by the open sliding door. The fresh air wasn't enough. It would never be enough.

His head spun and cold crept up through his feet from where he'd stood in her shadow outside the lift. The shadow – the place pushing out through the shadow – was coming. It would bring that dimension of darkness to the world. No, he thought as he absently tied his sheets together and then secured one end to the rails of his balcony, that was wrong. It would take the world to darkness. Somewhere worse than darkness.

Torment.

He could hear screams echoing in his head. They travelled with the chill in his bones. He wouldn't go there. He couldn't. He thought of the woman. She'd been Torchwood then. But now she was the one bringing it. Delivering them all to evil. How could she not know? How could she not see what was coming? What she was doing?

Tears ran down his cheeks as he tied the other end of the short sheet rope around his neck and checked it was firm. It was the remembering. Something in the remembering. It had opened his mind. His vision was blurred and his nose was running, but he scrawled his last message across his shirt. Seconds later, he climbed over the side of the balcony and let himself drop.

Chapter Ten

'So you have something that belongs to us?'

Commander Jackson was standing behind a large desk that had three phones and two computers on it. Cutler couldn't help but think it was overkill if this was just a recovery operation. If that's what it was. How many people did Jackson have to answer to, that they needed a phone each?

'I think so,' he said, and tipped the suit out of the bag and onto the floor. 'One of yours?'

Jackson said nothing but came round to the other side of the desk and stared down. He was an imposing man, well over six foot and with the kind of barrel chest that only men approaching 60 who have spent most of their lives in peak physical condition could achieve. Commander Jackson might be a Department man now, but he was Army through and through. It was clear from his stance.

'Looks like it.' He picked it up and inspected something halfway down. 'Where did you find it? Must have been one of our boys getting drunk and playing tricks on someone. Hiding their equipment. You know the kind of thing. I'm sure your lot do it. They all need to let off steam.'

Cutler followed the Commander's eyes. He might have been making light of the suit's discovery off-site with his voice, but his gaze was focused. What was he looking for?

'Behind a bin at the back of Allen Street,' he said. He frowned as both his and the Commander's eyes halted. There was a small cut in the suit in the torso area. Cutler caught a glimpse of it just before Commander Jackson folded the suit up. He hadn't noticed it in the station, but then he hadn't been looking. He cursed himself quietly.

'There was no helmet,' he added. 'My officers are looking for that now.'

Commander Jackson smiled, as he placed the suit under his desk. 'Thank you very much for bringing this in. I'll find out who's responsible for the prank and make sure they're fully reprimanded for wasting police time.'

Cutler returned the smile. This hadn't been a joke between soldiers. He knew that and so did Jackson. Whatever was really going on, the Commander had no intention of telling DI Cutler about it. Could the cut in the suit have been from a knife? He thought again of the figure he'd seen casually strolling away from the site the previous morning. Perhaps he should tell Commander Jackson about that. He decided against it. They could all keep secrets.

'As long as that's all it is,' he said. 'A prank.'

'Of course. What else could it be?'

Someone rapped briskly on the door.

'Come,' Commander Jackson said, and then smiled again at Cutler. It was an impatient expression.

It was suddenly clear to Cutler that his visit was over. He smiled back. 'Well, I'll leave you to... whatever it is you're doing here.' He might have been hoping for an explanation of some kind on that point, but it was obvious he wasn't going to get one. A soldier saluted in the doorway and then strode to the Commander as if Cutler wasn't even there and handed him a piece of paper.

'I'll see myself out,' Cutler said. His hand was already reaching into his coat pocket for the cigarettes that had somehow come with him to work. The odd one couldn't hurt, surely? Not with the workload that was facing him today.

Through the open door he could see two suited men ducking through the white tarpaulin to reach the site beyond. He thought about the water tower that had stood there. *You could be invisible there*, he thought. *Just in that one spot*. The words entered his head out of nowhere and meant nothing to him. No, that wasn't quite right. They meant *something*, he just didn't know what.

'Detective Inspector?'

He'd been about to step out into the fresh air when the Commander called him back. His head was still momentarily filled with the sound of trickling water as if he were standing in front of the destroyed water tower that had been such a feature of Cardiff Bay.

'Yes?' He turned. Any light-heartedness that had been in Commander Jackson's earlier tone was now gone.

'Have you heard about these murders discovered this morning? Three bodies all with missing eyes?'

'It's my case, actually.' It was Cutler's turn to sound defensive. Andy Davidson had been right. The news stations must have been quick to report this morning's victims. 'Why?'

'When was the first one killed?'

'It's too early to say. And anyway, this is confidential...'

'Nothing's confidential from the Department. You know that.'

'Do I?' The two men locked gazes and then Cutler thought of the figure strolling out of the site, and the cut in the suit. If that had been caused by stabbing then whoever had left in the suit wasn't the person who had been stabbed. They could never have walked so casually if injured. Whoever had been attacked was the original wearer of the suit. What the hell was going on here? Janet Scott had been stabbed. And so had the three victims Davidson had told him about on the phone. He looked again at Commander Jackson. There was no point in holding back the information about Janet Scott – the newspapers would have it by now anyway.

'The first victim was killed yesterday lunchtime. Why do you want to know?'

'I want to see the bodies.' Jackson pulled his coat from the hook on the wall. 'Discreetly, of course. But get them to the mortuary as soon as possible. You can brief me on the way.'

Cutler almost laughed. 'I'm sorry, sir, but this is my case and you can't possibly—'

'With all due respect, it's not your case. Not any more. The Department will be taking over from here.'

Cutler stared at him until he realised that the Commander really wasn't joking. His fingers tightened around the cigarette packet.

'I'll have to call my superior officer,' he said through gritted teeth.

Jackson was already heading out of the Portakabin. 'Of course. He'll confirm what I've just said. We'll need you on board, of course. Even if it's just as a figurehead. Can't have the Department seen to be running the case. That would raise too many questions.'

As Cutler followed him out, his blood boiling, he had a few bloody questions of his own.

Chapter Eleven

Andy Davidson had spent at least forty-five minutes looking for DI Cutler before someone had mentioned trying in the gym. Even though his mind was on other things, it annoyed him that he hadn't thought of it. But then he never used the place and had forgotten it was there. Cutler, on the other hand, was a keen runner and often disappeared into the station's basement to use the weights room and the treadmill if the Welsh weather was too vile to hit the roads. The gym was a relatively new addition – a stress-relieving initiative by the top brass, apparently. Andy thought it had more to do with the brass wanting them all to get in better physical shape, and thus far he'd successfully avoided it himself. He had a naturally slim frame and despite his lack of regular exercise could still chase down a thief or a mugger when he needed to. He was buggered if he was going to spend his free time practising.

The building grew quieter as he took the stairs down. It had been a busy day and most people were still at their desks working upstairs. It was only

Cutler who had vanished, and Andy guessed that his boss wanted the gym to himself for an hour so he could vent his frustrations privately. He didn't blame him either. He'd never seen the DI so angry as when he'd shown up at one of the crime scenes – the toilet at the back of a late-night café – and told them all quietly to get the scenes processed as quickly as possible and to get the bodies to the mortuary. It was a contained rage.

Thinking about it, it seemed to Andy that Cutler was screwed either way. With the Department making him the front man for the case, he had to take the rap if the murders weren't solved, and still do all the talking to the press, but he was unlikely to be given any proper answers even if the Department did find out who was responsible. He shivered slightly as he pushed open the door to the changing rooms. Who were the Department, anyway? They weren't entirely military, but at the same time they weren't MI5 or MI6 style spies. They gave him the creeps almost as much as those bodies with the bleeding eyes did. He didn't like the thought that the two were linked. Not at all. There was nothing comforting about it. It was a bit like the old days coming back to haunt him.

Both the Department and the state of the bodies reminded him too much of Torchwood business, and that made his heart race with more than fear. Most of the time he could separate his day job from everything he knew about Torchwood and the awful events that had left Ianto dead and poor Gwen in hiding, but there were these strange murders and now these new developments he needed to tell Cutler about. Cardiff was going spooky again. He thought of the number stored in his brain – the only place he felt safe keeping it – and wondered if maybe he should call it and ask Gwen for help. Or at least find out if she'd heard of anything like this before. Especially as the contamination suit that had been found could only have come from the Hub site. But he couldn't call her. She had enough problems of her own. Plus, he still had moments of quite well-founded paranoia that first his unexpected promotion and now his sudden secondment to CID hadn't entirely been as a result of his own hard work but more as some kind of pay-off from above after everything that had happened with the children. The cool air didn't help his inner chill, and neither did the memory of those eyeless corpses.

Still, it wasn't as if either he or Cutler were going to have too much time to think about them for a while. That was now Department business, and as of an hour ago it looked like they had a whole heap of other trouble to investigate. Andy Davidson just wished everything hadn't abruptly gone quite so weird.

DI Cutler was standing in front of a locker, a towel wrapped around his waist.

'Sir?' Andy said. Cutler didn't look up. Steam billowed from a shower cubicle behind him as if he'd got out and forgotten to turn it off. Maybe he'd just needed to get his shampoo or something. Andy frowned. That was a lot of steam.

'Sir?' he said again. What the hell was his boss doing? Most of the lockers were empty and had their metal doors open. Cutler was moving slowly along the line and closing them. When he finished the first row, he bent forward and continued along the bottom.

'What are you doing, sir?' Andy went into the shower stall and fought his way through the steam to turn it off, the mist making his shirt cling to his back as the damp soaked it through.

Cutler had moved to the top row. 'It needs to be closed,' he muttered. 'It needs to be closed. Before it's too late.'

'What does?'

Finally, now that his sergeant was standing right behind him, Tom Cutler turned to face him. His eyes widened, surprised.

'Where the hell did you come from?'

'Um…' Andy shuffled slightly from foot to foot. 'I've been here a couple of minutes. What were you doing? What needs to be closed?' He around him. 'Apart from all the locker doors, apparently.'

Cutler frowned. 'What are you on about?' He picked up his trousers from the bench. 'Anyway, what are you doing down here? Do the Department need me to perform some tricks for them? Roll over and beg? Oh, no,' he sneered slightly as he pulled his clothes on, 'the DCI has already done that.'

'It's not to do with that.' Andy put Cutler's strange behaviour to one side. The DI seemed fine now. He must have just been mulling something over and got lost in his thoughts. He needed to stop seeing strangeness everywhere. The Torchwood days were done. 'Although Fellowes said the helmet turned up in one of the bins near the site. It's gone to the lab.'

'Good. What else?'

'Something odd's been reported. Two suicides. Quite nasty – one stabbed herself in the kitchen this morning while getting the family's breakfast and another hung himself over the side of his balcony after getting home from his night shift at work.'

'So?' Cutler said. 'Suicide's not our business.'

'I know but both of these left the same message. It just said, "I remember".'

'"I remember"?' The DI did up his shirt.

'Yeah. Weird, huh?'

'Well, we may as well take a look before the Department get on my back to deliver their press release for them like the dancing monkey I am.' He grabbed his jacket. 'Just what the hell has got into this city anyway? Multiple murders and suicides all within a matter of days?' They stepped out into the blissfully steam-free stairwell. 'And I'm still not happy about that suit that was found. I know the murders are Department business now, but I want to keep an eye on just how much they're involved, if you know what I mean.'

Andy Davidson followed him up the stairs and back to the general hubbub of the station. 'You think the Department are *involved*?'

'Who knows? But they know something. Whatever's going on here, it's got something to do with that site. I can feel it in my bones, Andy. Let's play their game and keep them close. I want as much access as we can get to the case.'

'And the suicides?'

'Yeah.' Cutler sounded bored. 'We'll take a look at those too. They'll be a good smoke screen while we keep an eye on Commander Jackson and his boys and girls.'

'Yes, sir.' Andy Davidson grinned. It was good to be busy, and working with DI Cutler could never be considered dull.

Chapter Twelve

It was a place between places. It sat between time and space and galaxies, unnoticed. A dimension of its own. Sometimes, those more corporeal, the stars, the planets and space had a sense of it. They thought they glimpsed it in the folds of time and perhaps they did. Where sentient life existed in the universe it became a thing unspoken; a shiver, a dark shadow, a touch of a sixth sense.

As the worlds grew older and civilisations came and went, each one had a name for it. All life could sense its existence, even if they had never seen proof. They could feel it in the darkness of night and the nightmares that came from time to time. They wondered if perhaps it could come for them in the long sleep after death. They knew it was waiting and they knew it wasn't empty in all the ways that they knew it existed despite no proof. Survival instinct, gut, superstition – all told of the extra dimension. The one that didn't belong, that was filled with everything you feared, everything thing that caused you pain. They all had a name for it.

Time had no place for it. Life and death did not exist. There were no planets and stars and moons and spaces between them. It was empty darkness, and yet it was not empty. It waited. It was hungry. As the other dimensions were aware of it, so it and its inhabitants were aware of them.

For most of eternity, the barriers held, despite the talk of monsters and demons and madness amongst those who had given the place so many names as the years flew by. Civilisations came and went. Stars burned bright and died. Time passed. Eventually, a young explorer sat out on the dark edges of space, so far from his home world, out near the new star of the nine planets. For a long time he just stared into what looked like a tiny rift in space.

He considered himself a clinical thinker and had no time for superstitions. The tiny cut in space over the third planet, so small his equipment had nearly missed it completely, had begun to fascinate him. Not for itself – but for where it could lead. He would show those at home that there was nothing to fear from that place of darkness and nightmares – if it even existed.

He studied the rift for a long time. The tiny planet below circled its sun several times as he sent in probes and measuring devices and studied the data they sent back. Finally he found it. He was sure. A measure of space completely other to anything he'd encountered before. A blip in the readings. Somewhere inside the rift was a doorway or a tear of some kind to a place whose physics were entirely different to their own. His heart raced. This was it. This was the moment and the place that he would come into his glory.

He worked carefully. How long such an unnatural opening would remain he couldn't determine. The forces of nature would be aligning to knit it back together. Such an unnatural thing could not be allowed to continue. Physics would be unbalanced should one leak into the other and physics was the one law above all others, no matter how the spiritualists argued otherwise.

When he was ready, he launched the remote viewer, as small an item as he could make it, slim and rectangular, into the rift, attached to a tiny drone. From within the safety of his own ship, he navigated it towards the cut in space and time. The rift itself, tiny as it was, was fascinating. There were things in it; items of debris from various cultures and civilisations, some of which he recognised and some he didn't. It was bigger on the inside than the tiny entrance suggested. One unnatural thing housing a gateway to another unnatural thing. He found that the idea made him shiver slightly and that caused him irritation. It was superstition to be afraid with no reason; and he was no spiritualist.

The remote viewer slipped from one dimension to the next and he turned on the monitor, his vast palms slick with nervous anticipation. For a long while, nothing happened. He slept. He checked his instruments. He tried not to feel disappointed, for that too was not the clinical way. He would simply have to try again.

He was sleeping when the screen came alive. It went from the blackness of simply being off, to a terrible darkness of something other. His mouth dropped open and his weighty arms flopped away from the control panels and to the sides of his command chair. He felt its hunger, the excitement of all the strangeness that lived – no, not lived – existed within, as it reached out back through the viewer and sought him out. He had what it needed. He couldn't tear his eyes away and cold sank in through his skin as the dimension tore into his mind for his fears and terrors and the things that woke him in the night when he was a child.

He wanted to cry. He wanted to scream. He wanted to turn his ship around and go home and shout to the world that the spiritualists were right and there were things worse than the endless sleep that faced them all. There was a blacker darkness than nothing and they should pray to nature and physics and each other that it would never find them.

He did none of those things. Instead, his eyes exploded as the dimension took him, and his body died, sitting in shit, in his commander's chair. The ship drifted for years, for a while sucked into the orbit around the sun, mimicking the third planet's movements, the rotting body and rusting ship looking on as life formed there and spread across its surface. As the law of averages would have it – if not the laws of physics pure that the young adventurer had once held so dear – the dead ship finally drifted into the rift and joined the debris there, not long in fact before the search vessel cruised by the small solar system so far from home.

They didn't pause for long and didn't see the tiny rift above the third planet. The young adventurer would not have come this far from home, they concluded, before turning back.

As the law of averages – which often proves to be the most reliable – would have it, the small viewing device finally slipped out through the tear hidden within the rift. But like its creator it wasn't unchanged by its experience. The unnatural had connected with it for too long, perhaps because its creator was endlessly tormented in the foul darkness. There was no screen waiting for it to be switched on and SEE. Just the hungry darkness.

Time passed and the small metal card drifted through the rift, until finally, as the law of averages would have it, the viewing device finally fell from the rift and to the third planet below, falling into the ocean. The third planet had grown and filled with life since the young explorer had paused above their skies. They too had been plagued with glimpses and fears of something beyond. They, like all the other civilisations, gave it a name and, like all the other civilisations, some laughed at it, and others believed it was what waited for so many of them when the quiet nothing of death came.

And all through the years, beyond the tear in the rift, Hell waited.

Chapter Thirteen

'Commander Jackson?'

The soldier had probably spoken his name more than once judging by the uncertain look on his face when Elwood Jackson looked up. He wasn't surprised. He'd been lost in the information the police had given him regarding the murders, and his head was swimming slightly. That they were committed by the same person who had killed John Blackman was clear, but who *was* that? All his staff were present and correct. Could one of them have killed Blackman and gone and dumped the suit in a back alley and then got back to the site and into their own, to make it look as if someone had killed him and left? Could anyone have done that without being noticed? He was angry enough that someone had been able to just walk out of the site with a suit on without being stopped or questioned.

They'd all got slack, that was what had happened. The operation had been going well and with little interest or interference from the rest of Cardiff, or indeed the country, and so those on duty weren't staying focused. Well, they bloody would do from now on, even if he had to drag them down to the mortuary and show them those awful dead bodies himself. Death itself didn't bother him, nor would he expect it to bother his soldiers – they were all experienced campaigners who had no doubt each seen horrific sights. But the unnatural quality of these deaths was disturbing. There was nothing earthy and gritty about them, and although they'd been told to expect 'interesting' finds on the recovery dig, this was something else. He was both looking forward to and dreading the pathologist's report on the bodies. He hoped there'd be an explanation for the eyes.

'What is it, Corporal?' He closed the folder and thankfully placed the dead in his top drawer. He'd looked at them enough for one day.

'The Department have sent over a new Liaison for you.' The young man stepped aside. 'Sue Costa.'

For a moment, Commander Jackson said nothing. He was too surprised. The woman in the doorway stepped forward and smiled, her teeth perfectly white. Her dark eyes twinkled in her face and he decided in that instant that she was quite beautiful; feline and languid perhaps, but beautiful. Her red shirt dress stopped just above the knee, and he couldn't help his eyes wandering down her slim body to the matching red heels at her feet. He was old, admittedly, but he wasn't dead. He could still appreciate a good-looking woman, and after the pictures he'd just been studying, she was a welcome relief.

'You look surprised to see me,' she said, still smiling. 'Sorry about that. You know what the Department are like. You should have an email somewhere saying I'm coming.'

'You're right,' he said. 'I wasn't expecting you. What exactly have the Department sent you for?' He glanced up at the waiting soldier. 'You're dismissed, Corporal.'

'Yes sir. We checked her on the way in, sir. She's cleared.'

They waited until the door was closed.

'These murders,' the woman said, taking a seat opposite his desk and crossing her elegantly long legs. 'The Department feel that it's probably best if I act as your liaison with the police while the investigation is under way. Thus far, the activity at this site has caused no problems with the general public, and should anyone suspect that perhaps someone involved with the work here is responsible – well – you can imagine.'

'Quite true.' Commander Jackson wasn't quite sure how to react. The request was perfectly reasonable, and yet he couldn't help but feel that some of his control was being wrested from him.

'You have a high profile in the city and the Department feel that the residents have grown to trust you – your military and war record certainly help that – and therefore they don't want that reputation damaged. Not while you still have so much more to do here.'

'That would make sense,' he said.

'You will still be doing all the behind-the-scenes work on whatever happened here and to those people in the city; I'll just be the go-between.' She smiled again. 'And I certainly don't intend to be drawing any attention to myself. I'll do what I can by phone. The rest of my job description is to be your Personal Assistant, which I should imagine will take up most of my time.' She glanced down at her watch. 'Perhaps I should start by getting you some lunch. I don't suppose you've eaten?'

'No...' He was about to say he wasn't hungry – looking at the pictures had killed his appetite for a while – but he found that perhaps he was. 'Actually yes, that would be lovely. The canteen on site isn't great.'

'Not a problem.' She was on her feet, her handbag casually over one shoulder. 'Cardiff Bay isn't short of places for food.'

'I'll get on to someone to get you a desk and a computer set up.'

'Thank you. Once again, sorry to have been a surprise.'

'A pleasant one, however,' Commander Jackson said.

After calling someone to get equipment moved in to the far end of his Portakabin, he checked his emails. She was right – there was one there, sent the previous day from some Department email address but not a name he recognised, stating that she would be arriving to assist him in a supporting role. He scanned it and then closed it down. Now that he was adjusting to the idea, having an attractive woman around wouldn't be such a terrible thing. He glanced over at the machine in the corner. At least there would always be fresh coffee.

Chapter Fourteen

Andy Davidson had been right. The suicides were certainly taking Cutler's mind off the Department taking over the murder case that he was pretty sure they were involved in. At least Commander Jackson seemed OK – or as OK as the military could be. He would never entirely trust anyone in a profession that required you to simply follow orders and never question anything. To an outsider looking in, there might not be that much difference between them, but policing was *all* about digging and questioning. What he trusted least was that the Department and Army were now in charge of a case that was probably caused by one of their own. How long would it be before the whole thing got brushed under the carpet and he was left as the scapegoat who couldn't solve the case?

Still, those were thoughts for later. For now, he had a different riddle on his hands. He tapped his pen on the desk as he frowned.

'You're right. This is odd,' he said.

'I told you.'

'So, we've got Andrew Murray and Rebecca

Devlin. Any more come in?'

'No.' Andy was standing alongside him and they both stared at the pictures of the dead taken when they were alive and vibrant.

'Rebecca Devlin was married with children and Andrew Murray lived alone. Different parts of town. He worked nights and she was a stay-at-home mum. No signs of depression? Any clues that they were about to top themselves?'

'None. Andrew Murray was a bit of a loner, but according to his parents and work colleagues he was happy that way. He night-managed a supermarket. Had worked his way up from shelf-stacking.'

'Thrilling way to spend your life,' Cutler said. 'I think I'd throw myself off a balcony too. But the woman... Mother of three? And killed herself while making the children's breakfast? That's the disturbing part. Why not wait until the house was her own? Why did she do it then?'

'God knows. The youngest child came downstairs first and screamed. That's when the husband got out of the shower and found her. He's in shock. She'd been talking about what to cook for dinner only fifteen minutes earlier. And then, *wham*, she's killed herself.'

'And they both remembered something. That's the key. They remembered something very suddenly. Did either of them have the radio on? TV? Anything that might have triggered a memory?'

Andy Davidson scanned the various sheets

of notes he and several constables had taken. 'No. Definitely not in Rebecca Devlin's case, and probably not in Andrew Murray's. He can only have been in his flat for a few minutes before killing himself. His shift only finished half an hour earlier.'

'And Murray doesn't have children, so it can't be connected to all that recent madness.' He looked over at his sergeant. 'The kids are all normal, I presume?'

'Yep, all three bright and healthy.'

'So it's not that.' Cutler's brain itched. There had to be a connection. 'I want you to check their schools – see if they went to the same ones – it's a long shot but who knows, maybe there's a link there. Also, I want to know if either of them have been caught in any kind of natural disaster, here or abroad – something that could cause post-traumatic stress. Oh, and check the family histories too. Maybe their parents knew each other. Maybe the thing they're remembering is something from their infancy. They're only a year apart. It's possible.'

'Yes, sir.' Andy Davidson was dutifully scribbling it all down, and Cutler was once again grateful to have been given such a competent sergeant to work with. They might be clutching at straws, but Davidson knew that didn't need pointing out. And sometimes it was the straws that saved you.

'The message. What do you make of it?' Cutler asked.

'How do you mean?'

'It's strange for final words. No apology. No love for those left behind. It's almost a message.'

'Or some kind of warning. Or threat.'

'Threat?' Cutler asked.

'Yeah, but I can't put my finger on why. They're like some kind of accusing finger. Whatever it is they remembered, it wasn't good.' A shadow passed across the sergeant's face and Cutler was surprised by it. What dark memories did he have?

'Well, there's a link somewhere between them that we're not seeing. There's no way this could be a random coincidence. I don't care how many monkeys are typing in a room somewhere.'

'Sir?'

'Don't worry. Just a saying.' He stared at the smiling face of Rebecca Devlin. She had been a pretty woman with an open smile. Something triggered her that morning, just as it had for Andrew Murray. He sighed and his mind ran over their morning. Murray finishing work and heading home. Rebecca Devlin getting up and getting her family ready for the day.

'Who died first?' he asked.

'Rebecca Devlin. Andrew Murray was approximately an hour and a half after.'

'And how did he get home from work?'

'He walked.'

Something was bugging him. Even if they couldn't figure out what the two had remembered, the trigger had to be somewhere. 'What had Rebecca Devlin done since getting up?'

'Not a lot according to the husband. They talked in bed for a few minutes when the alarm went off – usual stuff, when he was getting home, what the kids had on. What to have for dinner. He got in the shower and she went downstairs to start getting breakfast ready.'

'And downstairs? What did she do?'

'Well, there was cereal on the table, and bowls. And she'd put eggs on to boil. They were boiling over when her husband got to the kitchen.'

'That's it?' There had to be something more.

'Oh – and she put the rubbish out. The husband was upset by that because it was his job to do it and he knew she'd be mad at him because she hated doing it.'

Cutler stared at his sergeant. 'So, she went outside?'

'Just for a couple of minutes.'

'Where are the bins? Front or back?'

'Front. By the pavement.'

Cutler stopped tapping his pen. 'That's it then. She must have *seen* something out there that triggered whatever was so terrible that it made her kill herself.' He paused. 'And then, on his way home from work, Andrew Murray saw the same thing. Or person.'

'Bit coincidental, don't you think?'

'Maybe. But not necessarily.'

'I don't get it,' Andy said.

'Think about it. These two killed themselves, but for all we know whatever they *remembered* could have happened to a hundred people – or a thousand. If that was the case, then two people seeing the same trigger would be less of a coincidence. Get someone chasing CCTV cameras of Andrew Murray's route home, and anything near where Rebecca Devlin lives. Let's see if we can find something or someone to connect them. Maybe the same car, hopefully the same person.'

'I'll get some people on it. But it's going to take a while. And the DCI won't be happy – a lot of manpower for suicides.'

'He owes me for rolling over so nicely for the Department.'

'Which reminds me,' Andy said. 'The press conference is in an hour. I'll get on to Commander Jackson's people and see what they want you to say.'

'What they want me *not* to say is more likely.' The phone on the desk rang out, and Andy grabbed it and listened before holding it out for Cutler. 'It's Spanton. They've got some results in.'

At least the pathologist had called him instead of going direct to the Department. That was something. Cutler pressed the loudspeaker button. 'What have you got, Doc?'

'Nothing simple, I'm afraid. Although all the victims suffered a stab wound that was direct into an organ – mostly the liver – that's not what killed them.'

'What do you mean?' Cutler and his sergeant exchanged a glance. 'Have you figured out what happened with their eyes?'

'Figured out would be stretching it. I haven't

seen anything like this before, and the bodies are heading off to some Department lab for further testing, but it looks as if their eyes burst due to sudden pressure from a massive brain haemorrhage. And I mean massive. To put it in layman's terms – in fact, I'm not sure there even *is* a medical term for something like this – their brains were pulped. All of them.'

Cutler ended the call and looked at Andy, who'd paled slightly.

'Did he say "pulped"?'

'Yep,' Cutler nodded. 'But I'm guessing that's one piece of information that won't be going into the press conference.' He looked back up at the board with the suicides' pictures on it. What the hell was going on in Cardiff?

Chapter Fifteen

At night she could breathe. She could be herself. All day she'd smiled and flirted with the old Commander and made him feel at ease with her. She'd discovered nothing useful as yet, but she would. Today wasn't the day for that. She'd shed her red dress and changed into fitted black trousers, high-heeled boots and a strappy top before heading back to the bars of the Bay. Her eyes glittered with sparkly shadow and her lips were filled in red.

She felt powerful. Gone were the insecurities she'd felt before – the suspicion that she had never been *good enough*. That she'd been so easily replaced by someone *better*. Well, as it turned out, that was all a matter of perspective. She'd almost killed that replacement, the sickly sweet Miss Cooper last time round, and where were all of the glory boys of Torchwood now? Nowhere to be seen and probably dead in the rubble. That darkness was theirs now. Let them enjoy it. She traced her fingers along the wall outside one bar and behind her a small piece of her shadow detached itself and lingered there.

Her stride was long and easy, the roll of her hips sensual as she made her way to the bar. She smiled brightly at the young man in a red T-shirt who was behind the bar, Jason according to his name badge, and ordered herself a bottle of beer. She took a long swallow, straight from the bottle, and let her eyes wander around the room. She'd killed someone for the thing inside her down a side street between the last bar and this one, now she wanted someone for herself. The beer buzz was good, and she rolled her head around her neck slightly as she leaned back and rested her elbows on the bar, forcing her torso forward. It was a sexy, predatory pose, echoing the strength she felt inside. She glanced down to check her vest top hadn't risen up to reveal the pulsing light beneath her skin. She was sure it had faded somewhat, anyway; it had looked like it in the shower.

What did that mean, she mused, as she met the gazes of several men, evaluated them, and then moved on. Was the viewing device stopping working? She didn't think so, not given the way she'd felt that vast dimension sucking her last victim in. She'd felt the horror without and the horror within. *I've got something to show you...* She'd heard herself saying the phrase every time but wasn't sure where it came from. It was more likely that the device had moved further inside her. Maybe the explosion hadn't just activated it, but had dislodged it too. That should probably frighten her, but she found that it didn't. So far, the device had proved very accommodating to her. Rescued her from the darkness of death and turned her into its instrument instead. They were a team, and long may it last. She smiled slightly and swallowed more beer.

She remembered the gasping terror of the man she'd just killed – the way his eyes had looked before she'd slid the knife in him. When they'd started to swell and she could see her own reflection clearly in their terrified expressions. It wasn't her they were seeing, though. It was something beyond. Something on the other side of her eyes and a dimension away. What was it they saw, she wondered? And for how long? She smiled. It didn't matter to her. She was *Death*, the deliverer – what the awful, unnatural eternal blackness did with the essence of those people afterwards wasn't her business. She had suspicions though. When she felt it opening up inside her, she was sure she could hear distant sobbing and cries for help. Her smile faltered slightly. Was it possible that there was a place worse than the empty darkness that came with being dead? The nothingness? It didn't matter, she decided, fighting the sudden shiver; she had no intention of going there. Her eyes rested on a man in the corner of the room, sitting on his own, and sipping from a bottle of beer like her own. After a moment, he sensed he was being watched and looked up and smiled. Suzie felt her mood lift. He'd do. He'd do very nicely.

He got to his feet and headed towards her. His dark hair was gelled, but not too much, and his grin was wide and handsome. He was about the same height at Captain Jack Harkness, too. The eyes were darker, nearer grey than Jack's blue, but she could get past that. This murder would be for herself, not the growling thing that looked through her, and the man's resemblance to her Torchwood boss would just add to her pleasure.

'Can I buy you a drink?' the stranger asked. His accent was Welsh, but in Suzie's head it was smooth American.

'Sure.' She drained the bottle, letting her lips linger at the edges of the glass as her eyes flirted with his, no orbs of dark sucking him in, only her own seductive brown. 'Or, we could go back to mine,' she said. 'I've got beer there. And it's less crowded.'

The man's grin stretched wide as if he couldn't believe his luck. As they headed towards the door, Suzie wondered if later on he'd see the irony. She slipped her hand in his and led the way.

Jason kicked the side door of the bar open and put the box of empty bottles down on top of the stack that was forming there, ready for collection the next day. He looked down at his red shirt and sighed. Great. One of the bottles couldn't have been entirely empty and had leaked part of its sticky contents over him. It was getting quieter inside, so he lit a cigarette and enjoyed the cool breeze on his face. As jobs went, it wasn't a bad one. There were worse ways of earning some extra money through Uni, even if it didn't pay loads.

There were always plenty of girls, and most of his shifts were with Sean, and they had a laugh.

He leaned against the wall and blew out a long stream of smoke, watching it get caught on the light breeze and sucked into the night. His mind drifted to the essay that was due in tomorrow that he hadn't even started yet, and the party he was going to at the weekend after work, and what clothes he should bring to change into, and was there anywhere he could grab a quick shower without having to go all the way home.

He frowned slightly as his gaze drifted to his left, to a point further along the wall, and the party and the essay were momentarily forgotten as it snagged his attention. What was that? He stood up and walked over to where the black patch was spread unevenly over the bricks. He couldn't even *see* the bricks underneath it. It was night, but the side street was well lit from a security light above the staff door, and the rest of the wall was clearly red, the mortar between the bricks visible. Not in the patch though. That was simply black with no sense of texture to its surface.

He took another long drag on his cigarette, and leaned in closer, his eyes searching up towards the second floor of the building, and then down to the pavement. Whatever it was, it was coming from neither end. The patch had simply formed in the middle. What was on the other side? Could it be some sort of oil or mould coming through from an internal problem? Rational as that sounded, he knew it wasn't true. This was something completely different.

'Jason?' Sean called from the door. 'I've done last orders. You having a fag?'

'Yeah,' Jason muttered. 'I'm over here. Look at this.'

More light had spilled out from the open doorway and it served to make the complete blackness of the patch stranger.

'What?' Sean sounded impatient. 'Let's get cleaned up first. I want to get home. I've *still* got a hangover from last night. I need sleep.'

'This patch,' Jason said. 'It's odd.' Something growled and cracked in the darkness, a soft almost-heard sound, but it still made Jason jump slightly.

'Jason, come on! Stop dicking around.' Sean snapped, his figure blocking the light as he stepped outside.

'OK, OK.' Jason had had enough of looking at the patch anyway. Something about it disturbed him. It reminded him somehow of that clown from that Stephen King book, the one with the sharp teeth and angry eyes that dragged kids down into the drains. Just looking at the patch of black made all his childhood fears seem real. He swallowed, and his mouth was dry. 'Sod it,' he muttered, and went to stub his cigarette out on the hidden bricks.

But there were no bricks. His arm slipped into the black.

'Sean?' he said. *It was so cold and so terrible and there were things in there, things that weren't things but they wanted to play with him anyway, all the things that he'd ever suspected had lived in the night, just out of sight, and there were screams and sobs of eternal torment and he could feel them running up his skin and soon his skin would be gone...*

'Sean?' he said again. His voice was soft and childlike and full of dread. Something tugged at one of his fingers and he let out a short yelp. There would be no essay. There would be no party. 'Sean, help me. Help me.' Something yanked him from the other side and half his body disappeared. He started to cry. He had a feeling he was going to be crying for a long, long time.

'What the...' Sean was standing in front of him, his eyes wide, and Jason stretched out his arm.

'Please! Please! It's got me! I don't want to go there! I don't want...'

And then the blackness sucked him in whether he wanted it or not.

'Jason?' Sean whispered into the quiet night. 'Jason?'

Neither the breeze, nor the blackness, gave him any reply.

'I knew a man that couldn't die once,' Suzie said quietly. 'I shot him right through the head. Just before I killed myself, actually.' She smiled. 'I suppose from your position that would sound like neither of us was too skilled at dying, but for me it was different. I was dead. Properly dead. Until they brought me back.'

The man tied to the bed whimpered and she saw his breath blow his cheeks out as he gasped and panicked behind the masking tape. His grey eyes weren't so flirtatious now. She let her own gaze drift away to a blank spot on the wall beyond.

'It wasn't so bad the first time. It was bad, don't get me wrong, but I'd only been gone three months. I'd only cracked the surface of nothingness. If I'd known then what I know now, I'd have left Dad till later and just got that silly cow somewhere quiet until the whole business was finished.' She gently stroked the man's sweating hairline, and ignored his flinch away from her. 'Hindsight, eh?'

'The second time was different. It was years. Years in the nothing, of being nothing. You know, when I woke up down in the vault, I didn't know who I was. That's how long I'd been gone. I didn't know who I was, what life was, anything. Can you imagine? To have been that long dead that you forget the brilliance of all this? Didn't remember a thing. Until I killed that man and stole his suit. Then it all came back to me.'

The man on the bed froze for a second, and then his struggles became more vigorous. Suzie didn't pay any attention. He wasn't going anywhere. She wrapped her dressing gown around her. The sex had been good. She'd enjoyed it, even if Owen's face had risen unbidden behind her eyes every time she closed them. The ghosts would fade. Once she'd got into the Commander's computer and found out exactly what had happened to them all, then she could perhaps start to sleep easily.

Or in fact, sleep at all.

'The problem with remembering life,' she spoke quietly, leaning forward and resting her chin on his chest, 'is that it makes you unable to forget death. I won't be nothing again. I can't be. To be nothing is terrible.' She let out a long, deep sigh. 'I don't know why I'm telling you all this. You'll find out for yourself soon enough. It's just nice having someone to talk to. Haven't had that for a while.' She laughed slightly. 'And it's not as if you'll be gossiping about me.'

She picked up the kitchen knife from the table beside the bed, and tears rolled down the cheeks of the panicking man. 'It's not the same as the one I used to use, of course,' she said, holding it up and turning it this way and that so the soft lighting made the steel glint. 'That one was very special. But then I'm not killing people to bring them back this time. And I suppose once a knife girl, always a knife girl.' She stroked his head again. 'This could be worse, you know. I could be letting the thing inside me have you. I have a feeling that going there would be like having this,' she carved a soft shallow line down his naked chest and watched the crimson ink spill out as his back arched and he screamed behind his gag, 'going on for ever and ever.' She paused in her work and looked into his eyes. 'As it is, this is just for me. I want to see someone else panicking as they have to say goodbye to all this and become nothing. It makes me feel better. Who says killers don't know their own motivations?'

She raised the knife again. 'Yes, I did know a man that couldn't die. Sadly for you, although you do look a little like him, you're not that man. This is your death. I am your death.'

She went to work.

Chapter Sixteen

Cutler had woken up just before dawn, and although he felt as if he'd slept fine, it took a couple of minutes before he figured out that maybe he'd had at least a short burst of sleepwalking activity in the night. It was more subtle than the taping up of his drawers and cupboards had been, but it appeared that at some point in the night he'd got up and closed every door in the flat; the bathroom, kitchen, lounge and his bedroom door. All shut. He never shut them, not even the bathroom door – who did that who lived alone? What the hell was he trying to tell himself?

The air was crisp outside, and once he'd showered and dressed – fighting the urge to close all the doors again before he left – he headed for the Bay, enjoying the clear streets as he drove in the almost light of the breaking day. He parked and stopped for a takeaway coffee before leaning against a wall and watching the excavation site. He didn't get as close as normal – his face was a known quantity there now, and the last thing he needed was Commander Jackson asking questions about why he was stalking the site – but he was close enough to see that there were more soldiers guarding the barriers than previously, and they all looked alert. No one in there was taking any chances.

Lighting a cigarette and inhaling hard, he wondered about the building the Department and Army backup were so carefully going through the wreckage of. Nothing was that hush-hush and smiley without there being something dangerous at the heart of it. And the site was connected to the murders. No one was denying that. The question was, did something at the site cause someone to go mad and go out killing? And how did you get someone's brain to turn to mush from the inside anyway?

He let his thoughts drift away from case practicalities as he smoked and drank his coffee. Slowly, light claimed the sky in orange and red streaks that faded to blue. His hands were cold and he found that, once the cigarette was gone, he'd been taking the lid from the coffee cup and then replacing it, over and over. He checked his watch, and with a sinking feeling realised it was time to get to work. It felt like he'd been standing there for five minutes, but nearer to an hour had passed. The water tower flashed behind his eyes again. The water tower and the greatcoat and a terrible sense of sadness and self-loathing. He stood up tall and shook it away. What the hell was wrong with him?

He smoked another cigarette in the car on the

way to the station. For a non-smoker, two cigarettes before 8 a.m. was pretty good going, he had to admit that, even if he refused to acknowledge that the old habit was back. He wasn't even aware of making any kind of decision to smoke again. It had just seemed to happen.

He strode into the station as if a purposeful step could make the weirdness that had taken hold of both him and the city vanish, taking the steps two at a time.

'You don't understand...' A young man was talking loudly to the desk sergeant. 'He just bloody disappeared. Into the wall. His name is Jason. Jason Wentworth. You need to come and—'

'Sir?' The sergeant held his hand up to pause the young man in his flow and grab Cutler's attention.

'Yep?'

'Can you call the lab? Forensics just rang through for you.'

'You need to come and look at the wall! He just disappeared into it! Aren't you listening to me?'

Cutler looked at the evidently distressed young student and then at the sergeant. Great. More craziness in the streets of Cardiff. 'Is there a problem here?'

'Yes, I—'

'No,' the desk sergeant cut the man off, 'no, there isn't.' He leaned on the counter, looking very much like a kindly uncle or grandfather. 'Look here, son. You go home and sleep off whatever it is you've taken last night, and if your friend is still missing tomorrow, then come back here and we'll try again. Are you sure he didn't just go off with a nice young girl?'

'No, I told you...'

Cutler gave the sergeant a conciliatory smile and then left them to it. He had his own strange fish to fry.

Andy Davidson was right behind him and, as the sergeant got the coffee on and checked his emails to see if they'd got anything on the CCTV checks for Devlin and Murray's surrounding areas, Cutler took a call from the lab. He wondered if now that the Department were involved they'd worked through the night. Maybe some good could come from having a case steamrollered after all.

'What have you got for me?' he asked.

'As you can imagine, there's a lot of trace to go through.' It was Abbie Trent on the line and that filled him with some confidence. In her mid-fifties, a hardened drinker – but never a drunk – and a survivor of three failed marriages, Dr Trent had moved down to Wales from Liverpool a couple of years before. She was good – probably one of the best – at her job, but her lifestyle and clear disregard for authority had never let that be acknowledged. If she was running tests on the crime scene evidence, then Cutler doubted anything would be missed. Trent might be belligerent, but she was thorough.

'Spanton has sent over what they got from the bodies, so we've been going through that first, along with the clothes. I wish at least one of these people had invested in a clothes brush. They're all covered in fluff and fur and all kinds of stuff.'

'I know it's going to take a while,' Cutler said. His heart sank slightly. If Trent had called just to let him know they were in for a long haul, then he could have done without it. He *knew* that. 'Just do what you can.'

'Oh no,' Trent said, surprised. 'We've got something. I wouldn't be bloody calling before eight in the morning if I hadn't. I'd be at home, in bed. Or at least having whatever slop they're serving for breakfast in the canteen here.'

'What have you got?' Cutler said.

'Hair. There were hairs from the same person on two of the victims. One was dark and the other was a slightly lighter colour but they're both from the same person.'

'Did you get a DNA match from it? Have we got anything on the system?'

'Ah,' said Dr Trent. 'This is where it gets interesting.'

And she was right. It did.

Chapter Seventeen

Suzie had been up early and got showered and dressed, making sure to step around the mess in her flat. She'd clean it – *him* – up later, but there wasn't any hurry. It wasn't as if he was going anywhere. And she had the spare room to sleep in, if the urge to rest took hold.

Commander Jackson had a meeting at eight off-site and she took the chance to dig around his computer. She ran an attack on his password and was in within minutes. It was time to find out exactly what had been going on during her recent trip into the nothingness of death. She didn't bother looking at the files regarding the excavation. She knew what was going in there – retrieval of alien artefacts and devices. That much was clear. Where they were all headed, she wasn't sure, and she found that she didn't much care. Not this morning, anyway. She didn't have long, and her primary objective was to satisfy her curiosity about the rest of the Torchwood team. She needed to know if there was anyone out on the streets of Cardiff that was going to recognise her face.

Within twenty minutes she was absorbed. Toshiko and Owen were both dead, within minutes of each other from what she could see. Her mouth twisted into a sour smile. Poor little Toshiko Sato, got to die with the man she wanted, even if she was the only woman he'd never shown any interest in getting into bed. She dug deeper, lost in the files on the 456. How the mighty fell, she mused, as she browsed the documents. So the government had ordered the destruction of Torchwood and the assassination of the team in order to cover up its own deal with the aliens. Torchwood, like anyone else, was expendable. A small twinge of anger surprised her. So Toshiko and Owen and all those who had gone before them had died for nothing. *She* had died for nothing. You gave your soul when you joined Torchwood, and this was how they'd been repaid. Jack had been blown up and buried in a concrete grave, rescued by his ever faithful – and soon to be dead himself she noted from his file – Ianto and her own replacement, Gwen Cooper. It irked her that Gwen was still alive out there somewhere. She would have to be the one that had bloody survived, wouldn't she? Perfect Gwen Cooper, everyone's favourite.

Her eyes fell on the conclusion of the 456 saga and her smile spread. Well, well, well, the great Captain Jack Harkness had sacrificed his own grandchild to save the world. She bet that hurt. His pride as much as his heart. Being a child-killer wouldn't sit well with his reputation or his own inflated opinion of himself. Bitterness rose like bile in her chest. She'd shot him. She'd killed him. It was just sod's law that Jack couldn't die. He probably saw it as some kind of noble burden he had to bear instead of a gift.

'Do you want kids one day, Suzie?' Jack leans back in his chair and studies her, thoughtfully. He's very handsome, she'll give him that. Her skin tingles when he looks at her. She'll never sleep with him though. She knows that, on some level. Captain Jack Harkness likes Suzie, but he'll never love her. She's not special enough.

'Doesn't really fit with our line of work,' she smiles, deflecting him. 'Long hours chasing aliens followed by,' she lifted her beer, 'a couple of hours winding down. Not really designed for being home in time for bath and bedtime stories.'

'You'd make a great mum,' he says. He's sipping water. She wonders if he'd find her more attractive if he had a beer or two. She'd like to sleep with him. She's thought about it. It would be different to being in bed with Owen, that much was certain.

'I don't come from good parenting stock.' The sentence is out before she realises that it's more than a thought, and her shoulders tense. Her life is her private business. One day she'll make sure she gets even with her dad, but for now there is no need to share. She doesn't need anyone's sympathy. 'Anyway,' she says, 'Torchwood is my family now.' She smiles, but he remains thoughtful.

'You're good at this job, you know,' he says. 'Better than most I've seen, and trust me, I've seen

a few. But,' he leans forward, resting his arms on his knees, 'you need to have more than just the job. You need a life. Something to keep you grounded.'

'Why?' she asks. 'So when I die some poor sod will be left wondering what's happened to me as all my possessions get carted off and stored in boxes in one of those lock-ups? Like we did for Ben Brown?' She shakes her head. 'It's not for me. Anyway, you're not so different. What do you have outside of the job? You don't have a family. You spend all night in the Hub, or standing on top of it staring at the stars and thinking about God knows what.'

His face darkens slightly and she wonders if she's touched a nerve. She knows so little – they all know so little – about the handsome American that they follow into danger at the drop of a hat. Torchwood. She loves it. She really does. It's given her life purpose. Until that incident with the alien computer virus that downloaded into her work mainframe, she'd simply drifted. She could have drifted into the Rift itself for all she cared. She'd felt like nothing. She'd believed she was nothing. Technical genius she might have been – able to get into any system presented to her, but she was as dead as the machines she managed.

'Torchwood saved me,' she says softly. She doesn't look at him as she speaks, but down at her beer bottle where her fingers are pulling the label free. 'It brought me back to life. This is the best job I've ever had.'

She remembers the sheer thrill of that first alien encounter. Feeling that something was wrong in *the system even though no one would believe her, seeing Jack and sweet Ben Brown, now in cold storage, investigate it and knowing, just knowing, that there was something special about them. That they were people she belonged with. People that didn't fit inside the world just like she didn't. She was the one who realised when the virus downloaded into her boss. It was she that had captured it. If it wasn't for her, her old boss would have been dead, and not pleasantly too. At least he couldn't remember his agony. Sometimes, when she remembers what a smug, smarmy bastard he was, she wishes he could have just a little part of his memory back. But hey, you couldn't win them all, and her clear thinking had got her a better job.*

'I don't need any more than this, Jack,' she squeezes his knee. 'I really don't.' He leans forward and kisses her gently on the cheek. 'One day you will, Suzie Costello. One day we all need something more than this.'

He sounds so sad and she wonders if he's as damaged as she is underneath all that easy charm and the bright smile. She almost asks, and then decides against it.

'Shall we go back to work?' she says. 'I'm sure I can smell Weevil.'

He laughs suddenly and she can't help but join in. She loves this. She really does.

Logged out of Commander Jackson's computer, Suzie sat back in her chair, surprised to find how much she was trembling. They hadn't cared about her. They'd bloody *killed* her. How could reading about them have affected her so much? It was a good thing that they were all gone. Torchwood on her tail was something she really didn't need; she had a history of coming off badly against her erstwhile colleagues. Still, she thought, taking a deep breath and steadying her nerves, sometimes you couldn't fight the memories – the good as well as the bad. Gunshots echoed in her memory. Her shooting Jack. Jack shooting her. Her shooting herself. She could safely say that things hadn't ended well for her and Torchwood – they'd turned out to be a family that hated her as much as her own one had.

She smiled. She'd had the last laugh with her father and she was having it again with Torchwood. Jack and Gwen were on the run and the others were dead and here was she, once again back from the dead. She checked her watch. The Commander would be back at any moment and she needed some fresh air. Time to have a little dig around for any new files on herself – she'd destroyed all the early ones but there was bound to be a new one with basic information after her last visit – and then to fetch lunch like a good little girl.

Chapter Eighteen

'Both hairs come from the same person,' Cutler said, trying to keep his focus on Commander Jackson rather than his gorgeous new assistant. And she *was* gorgeous, there was no denying that. She had eyes you could drown in and they were focused on him. Was it his imagination or did she feel the same sudden rush of chemistry that he did?

'So, you've found the killer?'

'Not exactly.' Cutler shook his head, turning his attention back to her boss. 'You may have to do that. When our forensics people ran the DNA through the system all they got back was that the result was classified. Even the commissioner couldn't get a result when he tried this morning. Whoever this is, it looks more like one of yours than a civilian.'

'Well, that would fit in with the missing suit,' the woman cut in. She was well spoken with no hint of an obvious accent. She smiled and Cutler was sure there was a slight tease in it. 'To be honest, did you expect anything different? I'm sure ever since the Department declared an interest, you've been pretty sure that any evidence would lead you here.' She held out a slim hand. 'I'm Sue Costa, by the way. The Commander's new liaison. I look somewhat less obvious than a soldier, we hope.'

'Tom Cutler. And yes, you do.' Somewhere in the background noise, Cutler was aware that the Commander was apologising for not introducing them and saying something about not being used to having an assistant that wasn't an invisible corporal or squaddie, but he wasn't listening. Sue Costa's hand was smooth and her skin cool, and it looked like if he licked it, she would taste of honey made from some exotic pollen. His heart thumped as they looked at each other. There was something about her – something that drew him in, just like the site drew him in. Something scratched momentarily against the inside of his skull, something dark and troubling. She squeezed his palm as if she felt it too.

He pulled his hand back and swallowed. He needed to get this under control. He was behaving like a teenage virgin, and it was a long time since he'd been either of those things.

'I appreciate that you want to keep all this in house, Commander,' Cutler said, 'and if it was just soldiers that were dying then I'd let you. But as there are ordinary people involved, could you please keep me in the loop. It's my neck on the line if there's no result. When you know who the hair belongs to, I would very much like to sit in on the questioning.'

'I'll have to check that with my superiors at the Department.' Jackson's face was giving him a definite no to the request, but Cutler hadn't lost anything by asking. It had told him that there were things they were doing at this site that they didn't want the general public – the police even – to know about.

'I will definitely give you a name, however,' the Commander acquiesced. 'And after that we can decide how best to proceed with progressing the case.'

Cutler almost laughed. *Progressing the case.* Covering up, is what the old man meant. No doubt the killer would be reported as having been shot during arrest and then the Army and the Department could do whatever they wanted with him. It didn't come as any surprise. Cover-ups were everywhere.

A barrage of sudden images assaulted him. *Night. A paedophile. He was sure. So sure. Wrecked lives. Something. Something other. Lies. And then all over again. Sad smile. Greatcoat. This is the twenty-first century when everything changes. Singing. Murder. Something other. Alien.* They were too quick for him to grasp. But the tangled memories scratched at his head again and he felt a sharp jolt of self-loathing and despair. What was that? That wasn't like him. He liked himself. He was a good copper. What was it he couldn't remember?

'Detective Inspector?' Commander Jackson stepped forward, worried. 'Are you all right? You looked as if you were about to pass out.'

The moment had gone, and the images with it, and aside from a trembling in his legs and coldness in his hands, he felt fine. He wanted a cigarette, but his head was clear. Whatever he thought he'd seen was gone.

'Yes, sorry. Long day.' He smiled awkwardly, aware that Sue Costa was studying him thoughtfully. 'I should have grabbed some lunch. I'll get something on the way back to the station.'

'Make sure you do,' Commander Jackson said.

'What are you doing this evening, Detective Inspector?' Sue Costa smiled at him, and for a moment he wasn't sure what to say. Was she asking him out on a date? Surely not...?

'The Mayor is having something of a bash,' she continued. 'Perhaps you'd like to come.'

Cutler's skin flushed. Of course. Work. How stupid *was* he? 'Email me the details, and I'll play it by ear. I'll have to see if we get any more bodies in. I doubt whoever's doing this has finished.' He kept his tone light. 'They might just have got better at hiding the bodies for a while.'

'The party would be a good place for us to talk without looking obvious,' Jackson said. 'It's better than you coming here every day. And I don't trust phones. Paranoid probably, but stay in this job long enough and a little paranoia will creep into your bones. The last thing we want is an eagle-eyed reporter spotting you calling in and then putting two and two together.'

'I'll do my best to make it,' Cutler said.

'I look forward to seeing you there.' Sue Costa's dark eyes were smiling and there was a promise in them, even if she wasn't aware of it herself. He was good with body language, it was part of the job, and he'd bet money that she was feeling the same pull towards him that he had towards her. How, he didn't understand, she was well out of his league, but he had no intention of pointing that out to her.

He was at the door when he turned, a thought striking him. 'You haven't had anyone in your team commit suicide over the past couple of days, have you?'

'No,' Jackson frowned. 'Why?'

'Ah, nothing. Just another heap of weird I'm looking into. Was hoping I could lay that one at your door too.' He grinned at the Commander and headed outside. His cigarette was lit before he'd got to the barrier, and God, it tasted good.

Chapter Nineteen

Commander Jackson's eyes were blurring from concentrated staring at the computer for so long. It didn't make any sense. He'd been quite surprised at the level of security around whoever the hair on the dead bodies belonged to. He'd expected any trace evidence the police might find to lead back to them – this had all started with the death of poor John Blackman, after all – but for even the Commissioner not to be able to access at least basic information was strange to say the least. The head of the police should have found a name, if nothing else.

Despite the tendency for the Department to be seen as something of a shadowy organisation, in reality it suffered the same bureaucracy issues as all companies. People needed personnel files and National Insurance numbers and bloody pensions and, on top of that, most people – even amongst those on site – were simply drones, for want of a better word. Even his own file had basic information accessible to some of the outside world. His name and rank, if nothing else.

He clicked the command button again, and got the same response he had on every attempt: 'File Deleted.' He frowned. Files were never deleted – in the movies maybe, but not in the real world. There were always copies somewhere in the sub-directories, because there always had to be an audit trail in order to know whose arse to kick when something went wrong. Thus far, he wasn't finding anything, though. Not even basic information.

'Is anything wrong?' Sue put a mug of fresh coffee on his desk.

Elwood Jackson managed a small smile. As surprised as he'd been by the liaison's arrival, he was finding that he enjoyed having a woman – one that didn't come in a uniform – around the place. She made a good cup of coffee as well as having somewhat amazing legs. The thought was sexist but he didn't beat himself up over it. He'd watched women die as bravely as men in battle and had a healthy respect for the workings of the female mind – he didn't see that there was anything wrong in admiring their form too. As far as he could tell, that was pretty healthy male behaviour.

'Nothing you can help with, I'm afraid. I'm still trying to get some kind of ID on Cutler's hair sample. So far it's proving tricky. You may as well head home for the afternoon. I'll need you in fine form tonight, because God knows, I'll be operating on minimum reserves.' He winked at her. 'I'm too old for late nights, and I've been a soldier too long for much polite conversation. You're going to have to take charge.'

'I can manage that.' She went behind her desk and turned her computer off. 'Are you sure you don't need me?'

'Absolutely.'

He waited until she'd left, and then picked up the phone. He needed to talk to the Department. There was something about this file that just wasn't right. He needed to know who had been deleting the records and when. He also wanted the back-up paper file – he didn't care if it took all night for someone to find it. DI Cutler wasn't the only one who wanted this person caught.

There was the inevitable round of questions that he didn't have the answers for – and he bit back from snarling that if he had all the answers he wouldn't need this information – and once he'd satisfied his alleged superiors that he wasn't just being remarkably stupid and his requests had been logged, he put the phone down and enjoyed a moment of blissful silence. He noted, with regret, that the coffee Sue Costa had brought him now had a cool film on its surface. He sipped it anyway, needing the caffeine fix to soothe his throbbing head and keep him awake. The phone rang moments later and he let it peal out twice before answering. So much for the quiet. His headache faded instantly. There had been another murder some time the previous night, not far from the site in the busy bar area of the Bay. The poor man, eyes exploded, had been found in an alleyway.

He put the phone down and contemplated

turning on the news to see just how much of a field day they were having with it. So far, although it had been impossible to keep the details of the missing eyes from the public, they'd covered it by saying that the eyeballs had been gouged out. There was no reason for anyone to suspect anything different – especially as the truth of the near-liquidised brains pressuring the eyes to explode wasn't exactly something that would spring to mind. They were also lucky that none of those who had found the bodies had lingered to examine them closely enough to see that gouging wasn't exactly what had happened. Most had simply screamed and run to find help. He didn't blame them for that either.

He took another swallow of the lukewarm coffee and left the small television off. His phone wasn't ringing so the police must have things under control, and he hoped that they'd go through Sue first, before coming to him. She seemed capable, and she and Cutler had definitely liked each other – he wasn't too old to notice that kind of chemistry working – and that wouldn't be a bad thing. He couldn't blame the DI for any irritation at the Department's intervention into his case. Cutler also looked bright enough to know that if the investigation failed to reach a successful conclusion, it would be Cutler who would get the bollocking. Still, that wasn't either of their problems for now, and at least Cutler was saved the knowledge that kept Elwood Jackson awake at night – that whoever, or *whatever*, was doing this to the good people of Cardiff might be using some kind of alien technology to do it. Nothing about that sat well with him. If he'd been in charge of this operation, he'd have had the whole place filled in. The human race had enough dangerous technology of their own, without playing around with things they couldn't possibly understand.

Chapter Twenty

'I think I like him, you see?' Suzie said softly as she stretched out on the bed. Her skin shivered against the chill of the sheets. The blood hadn't quite dried yet and they were still sticky and damp. 'I'll have to kill him, of course, but I do like him.'

She ran one finger down the cold, dead cheek. 'Is it still awful in there? Being nothing?' she whispered. The dead man no longer looked so much like Captain Jack Harkness. His face was grey and slightly waxy and his skin hung slackly around his jowls. Devoid of animation and quite a lot of his blood, it was like lying next to a stranger. They may only have known each other a few hours, but Suzie thought that she'd got to know him pretty well in that time. They'd drunk together, laughed together, had sex together, and then she'd tied him up and slowly killed him. You couldn't get much more intimate than that.

She prodded the flabby flesh of his cheek. Was this how she'd looked for all that time? The natural coffee colour of her skin faded to sickly blue as death and then the freezer took hold of her? She should have looked at the pictures before she'd deleted the file she'd eventually found that day, but she simply hadn't had the time. Not that it mattered. That Suzie Costello – the one who thought that everyone else was better than her – was long gone. This Suzie Costello had no intention of dying again any time soon. She wasn't sure that the thing inside would let her. She stared at the man whose name she had forgotten – if she'd even asked him for it – and although his mouth hung open, no answer came out. She had a moment of nostalgia for her old games with the Resurrection glove. This one really hadn't wanted to die – it had taken hours before he'd accepted it was inevitable. She'd quite like to bring him back just so she could put him through it again. If only briefly.

Bored of the silent company, she left the bed behind and swayed slightly to the music playing in the background, the CD now a few years out of date but still soulful. The bedroom curtains were open and, as night fell outside, her reflection moved with her on the sliding glass doors, the edges undefined and the blood that now streaked on her legs and arms intercut with streams of watery light from headlights and street lamps and boats out on the sea, all reaching upwards.

She looked like a ghost in the glass and that made her smile. Absorbed in her own image, she moved forward until she was pressed up against the cool surface. At some point after she'd come home, she'd stripped to her underwear and started putting on make-up, smearing red lipstick on and around her mouth until between that and the black rings of kohl she'd rubbed under her eyes, she looked like a strange demented clown. She stretched her face this way and that and tilted her head, studying the stranger that looked back.

She was a mad woman, that's what anyone would think were they to see her. Maybe they were right. After all, she had no recollection of painting her face so wildly, and the past few hours had been something of a haze, but she wasn't afraid. What was madness anyway, if not simply a matter of perception? She could shake the relaxing trance off when she needed to – to feed the vast existence within her, or to satisfy her own needs – and she wouldn't question it. She wasn't entirely human any more, that much she'd come to realise. Not only was she become *Death*, as the corpse on the bed could surely testify, but she was also a living gateway – a portal – to something else. A place more terrifying than the nothing she had inhabited. A place that had an insatiable curiosity about pain and was inhabited by demons and delights that no human could ever imagine. Sometimes she was sure she heard the echoes of screams of those she had sent there. They made her feel more powerful.

In the distance, the sea was a blanket of night. Perhaps that's what she was – a ferryman. A deliverer of the living to Hell.

Hell.

She shivered slightly as the haze fell away and

something inside her resonated with the word. The dimension recognised her thought. It had heard that word before and it recognised it as its name. The concept raged in the consciousnesses she had delivered to it, and the more she sent, the more clearly sentient it became. The dimension *liked* the name and all the word represented.

Her eyes blackened slightly, and she turned away from the glass. A small wave of panic trembled in her stomach but she drew herself up tall and shook the fear away as she strode towards the shower. She had become *Death* and now she held the gateway to an eternity of suffering within her. She would be the one to decide who got one fate and who another. How ironic that her relationship with death had started by trying to bring people back from it. Now that dream was gone. This power was so much *more* than that.

Under the glare of the bright lights in the bathroom, she wiped away the childishly applied lipstick and eyeliner and refocused on the night to come. Her hands paused in their work as she thought about the Detective Inspector. There was something about him... something that attracted her. It wasn't that he was overly handsome – he had that rugged thing going on but he wasn't exactly Brad Pitt – but she was drawn to him. She heated up when she looked at him, and it was only that afternoon when she'd been flirting with him that she'd realised just how cold she'd been since this new life began.

She turned the shower on and peeled off her

underwear. She'd have to kill him, of course. She knew that. He was too dangerous. The Department might have taken over the case, but Cutler was a relentless man. He wouldn't stop until he knew who was killing these people, and she couldn't afford to have him chasing after her once she left Cardiff. She couldn't stay here for ever, that had never been her plan, and soon even the Commander – stupid old-school gentleman that he was – would find links back to his new assistant.

Tomorrow her overseas accounts would be reactivated and she could leave both Sue Costa and Suzie Costello behind and head to her new life. She didn't think it was going to turn out exactly as she'd planned it when she'd put all her back-ups in place all that time ago – given her new propensity for killing, she may have to travel a lot – but she'd always wanted to see more of the world. She sighed as she stepped under the hot water. She'd start in Africa somewhere maybe, somewhere where the sun could beat heat into her. That would be perfect. Bad policing and beautiful weather. What more could she want?

She opened her eyes to reach for the shower gel, and it was only then that she noticed the change. Her hand froze in mid air for a moment. The red light beneath her skin had gone. Had it stopped working? Her heart raced. Would that plunge her back into the nothing? She took a deep breath. No. The viewing device was working. She could feel the vast black pit on the other side of her eyes. Where had the light gone then? As her breathing regulated, she grabbed the gel and squirted some into her hands. There was only one obvious answer. The device was no longer just on the other side of her skin. What she'd idly thought the previous night was right. The device had broken free and moved further inside her body. She was slightly surprised at how calm she felt. She had planned to have the device removed as soon as possible once she was away, but that might be trickier now, depending on where it attached itself next. Her heart? Her liver?

She tipped her head back in the water again. She could worry about that later. As it was, she was slightly comforted by knowing that the dimension needed her as much as she perhaps needed it. Taking the device out would mean risking going straight back to nothing if it was purely the alien technology that was keeping her alive.

As much as most of her now believed that she had a higher purpose and that she would be fine without it inside her, there was a very tiny part of her – that had to be what was left of the old, weak Suzie Costello who sought everyone's approval and thought she was worthless – that was still convinced that Death would claim her if she got too cocky and thought that perhaps she'd hugely underestimated the power of the dimension inside her. It was the same small voice that didn't want to kill the Detective Inspector. She would, though – she had no real choice. But, and she smiled and thought of the body still tied to her bed, there was no reason for her not to enjoy him first. To get the attraction out of her system. She rubbed the shower gel onto her naked body, and as she closed her eyes again, it was DI Tom Cutler's hands she was feeling.

Chapter Twenty-One

It wasn't the sort of party Cutler normally went to and, although he had too much quiet personal confidence to feel uncomfortable in the midst of all of Cardiff's social elite, he did find himself loitering in the corners of the vast, opulent room and just grabbing a fresh glass of champagne and a canapé as the trays passed by.

Despite having devoured at least a tray of various nibbles, his stomach still rumbled. There had been no time to grab any food after getting back to the station and then hearing about the fresh victim, and having to pass all that information onto the Commander as if he were some kind of obedient pet bringing a newspaper to his master. He'd even had to dress up for this occasion, so any chance he might have had for a quick burger had been taken up with a shower and digging out a half-decent suit from the back of the wardrobe. He also wanted a cigarette.

The police commissioner was in the gathering somewhere, but Cutler had simply given him a nod as they passed. He might be the only person the DI really knew at the party, but he'd rather skulk around on his own than spend the night talking to his boss and having to laugh at his jokes. He scanned the little clusters of men and women laughing and chattering over their drinks. He told himself he was just idly people-watching, but that wasn't the truth. Every time he saw a flash of brown curls his heart jumped a little. There was only one person he was interested in talking to tonight, and that was Sue Costa. He almost laughed at himself. He was acting like a teenager with a crush. Or if not a crush, then a very definite hard-on.

The party at the Town Hall was to celebrate the financial green light to the redevelopment that would restore Cardiff Bay to its former glory once Jackson and his team were done, and as Cutler strolled around the layout and shining model laid out on a table in a side room, he felt the strange lure of the site again. His heart thumped loudly in his ears. What was it about that place? What was it trying to tell him? Every time he was there or saw something related to it, he felt an annoyance at himself – as if he was being particularly stupid and not seeing something clearly before him.

'It will be good to have the Bay back to normal, won't it, Detective?'

Commander Jackson had appeared out of nowhere, or at least that's how it seemed to Cutler who'd been staring down at the model, lost in his own thoughts. He nodded slightly and then frowned and tilted his head. 'The water tower is back. They can get in and out without being seen.'

'What did you say?'

Cutler looked up, surprised. 'I didn't say anything.'

The Commander stared at him for a moment. 'Yes, you did,' he said, carefully. 'You said something about the water tower.'

'Did I?' Cutler's brain itched with information out of his reach, but nothing came to him. 'I liked the water tower. I just thought they might be replacing it with something new.'

Jackson continued to stare at him, but just as he looked as if he might say something more, they were interrupted.

'Hello, boys.'

She looked stunning, that was Cutler's first thought. The black dress was fitted to her like a second skin and he was pretty sure there was no room for underwear beneath it. It stopped just above her knee and her coffee-crème legs were bare down to her shiny high-heeled shoes.

'Looking good,' he said.

'Not so bad yourself, Detective,' Sue Costa smiled, her dark eyes twinkling playfully. 'I wasn't sure you owned a decent suit.'

'Oh, there's probably quite a lot you don't know about me,' he countered. They smiled at each other as if Elwood Jackson, in his full uniform, wasn't standing, slightly perplexed, between them.

'Well,' the Commander finally said, 'I'll leave you two to it. There are members of the press here, and I don't want them seeing us together for too long.'

Cutler nodded and so did Sue Costa, but neither of them looked his way.

'One thing though,' he continued, 'before I go. I've been trying to get some information on who that DNA sample belongs to.' That did make Cutler look up for a second. 'And?'

'Nothing so far. It's very strange. It would appear that the files relating to whoever it is have been deleted. I should know some time tomorrow by whom, but until then, I can't tell you anything.'

Cutler watched him carefully for a second. He had a good eye for a liar, and although he was sure the Department could lie with the best of them, Commander Jackson was an Army man at heart, not a Department player. If Jackson hadn't wanted to give him an ID, he'd just have told him it was classified and he'd deal with it. 'Let's see what tomorrow brings, then.'

The Commander headed away into the nearest small group of people, and Cutler wondered if he felt as out of place amongst the smugly successful business types and their tennis-playing, socialising wives and husbands as he did. More so, he imagined, but the Commander was smiling and listening intently to a silver-haired, pearl-laden, pink-lipsticked old dame as if he were born to it.

'Not your idea of a good night out, Detective?' Sue Costa was watching him thoughtfully, and they turned away from the architect's model and walked towards a quieter area near one of the large windows.

'I'm that easy to read? And it's Tom.'

She smiled and looked back at the party that was going on without them. 'They're all rather smug and self-satisfied, don't you think? Very pleased with themselves, even though none of them do anything particularly remarkable with their lives.' Her eyes had darkened thoughtfully, and for the first time he saw a softness to her. The flirtatious smile had dropped, and he found that she was more sensuous without it. 'They couldn't do what you do, or what the Commander does, or what I used…' Her voice drifted away. 'How is the murder hunt? Keeping you busy?' The edge was back in her voice and her back arched playfully. She was something of an enigma; he was learning that fast.

'If the past couple of days are anything to go by, then all I know is that one way or another everyone in Cardiff seems intent on dying at the moment.' His words didn't even feel like an exaggeration. Between the murders and the strange *I remember* suicides, there was an invisible pall hanging over the city. He'd also checked in with the desk sergeant over the student whose friend had gone missing, and he hadn't turned up yet either. He said he'd disappeared into a black shadow in the wall. It had just sucked him in. The desk sergeant had sniggered at that, but it disturbed Cutler. All three series of events were strange and that part of his brain that itched and dragged him to the site whenever he had a free moment was sure that somehow they were all linked. *The military coat. The easy smile.* He shook it all away. Tonight wasn't the night for that. Tonight he wanted to lose himself in Sue Costa.

'Whoever's committing the murders doesn't seem to want to either slow down or take their hobby elsewhere. But then, maybe when your boss can get to the files we'll know whether the killer is someone on his team or not.'

'Oh, I think we can be sure of that, don't you?' A knowing smile danced on her lips.

'Well, all the evidence certainly points that way. We found the suit. The Department stepped in. Ergo, they know they're to blame.'

'All that is true.' She leaned up on tiptoes, so that her face was at his ear. She smelled sweet and her breath was warm enough to send tingles running up his spine. 'But there was also the small matter of the first murder. It happened on site. The morning you found the suit.'

'What?' He turned to look at her, his eyes widening. 'Your boss didn't tell me that. Where's the body? What—'

She grabbed his arm to hush him. 'Don't look so obvious. It doesn't make any difference to the investigation. I just thought you should know. Think of it as a gesture of goodwill.' Her hand lingered on his arm. 'Of course if you tell the Commander you know about this, then I'll lose my job. So I'd rather you didn't.' She smiled. 'Not just yet, anyway. He wasn't Army or Department, I don't think. Just a geeky scientist boy. Nothing to look at. The kind of man that would probably have never really *lived*, however long he lived. Lovely eyes, though.'

Cutler looked at her, fascinated. Was she being intentionally cruel, or just observational? 'Can you get me his file tomorrow?' He leaned forward and spoke softly. His heart thumped hard. Was she feeling this overwhelming chemistry too? What was it about her? It was almost as if he recognised something of himself in her – something that he'd forgotten. As if she of all people could understand him, maybe better than he did himself. They *belonged* together. He knew it with a certainty. 'You are the liaison, after all. You scratch my back and I'll scratch yours.'

She sipped her champagne. 'It's not back-scratching that I've been thinking about all afternoon. Although we can do that too, if you like.'

Cutler was lost for words. She was absolutely gorgeous and that was a clear come-on. Even with the chemistry between them, he'd been sure he was going to have to work harder than that. 'Your place or mine?' he said.

'Yours.' She laughed slightly, as if at some private joke. 'Mine's a right bloody mess.'

They drained their glasses and no one noticed them leave.

Chapter Twenty-Two

Eryn Bunting woke up with a start, for a moment completely confused about who and where she was. She gasped for breath and fought a panicked scream that rose in her chest.

It was the darkness. The darkness was here. And there were unimaginable things *hiding in it.*

She sat up, blinking, and slowly the shadows took on familiar shapes: cupboard, chest of drawers, heap of unironed clothes in the corner. The faint glow from the street light a few metres down the road from her house made the edges of the heavy curtains a slightly lighter colour than the rest of the room, and she focused on it as her breathing steadied.

It was nothing, she thought. Just a bad dream. What did she expect after the strange couple of days she'd had? All those questions by the police and finding out someone had used her ID for something had left her feeling odd. Slightly violated and yet curious about a person she could only see as a doppelgänger of herself walking around Cardiff. The police hadn't told her what the woman had used her missing bank statement for, but it was clear from their interest that it had been something serious. Especially as it was a statement from so many years ago. Could a whole life be forged from one bank statement? She didn't think so – not that her knowledge of identity theft went beyond the basics seen on *Crimewatch* or being careful when using your credit card on the net. And surely if someone had made a whole life from that one document, she'd know about it by now? They'd have run up some kind of debt that would have shown on her credit record, surely? That was what people *did* with stolen identities, wasn't it? She'd bought her new car only last year, and nothing dodgy had come up then. She didn't know why it was stressing her so much. After all, as far as her own life was concerned, no harm had been done by the missing statement. She was normally a pretty calm and practical person, but something was niggling her. It was as if her brain was itching and the bank statement was somehow part of the cause.

Alan grunted in his sleep and rolled over, one arm stretching across her vacant pillow. It made her sad somehow. Why didn't he even twitch when finding the space empty instead of happily claiming it. Why didn't he miss her? Were they that comfortable with each other now? Would he notice if she was gone for ever, or would his clothes just spread from his wardrobe to hers and suddenly the toilet seat would be always in the upright position? Would anyone miss her once the dust settled?

The morbid quality of the thought wasn't like her at all, and she climbed out of bed to try and get away from it. Whatever dream had woken her must have disturbed her and she frowned trying to remember what it was. She'd been in the new deli down at the Bay, that was it. She'd been buying a sandwich, ham and coleslaw, exactly as she had done yesterday lunchtime. The dream had basically been replaying the events from her day. What was so scary about that?

She didn't turn the bathroom light on but sat on the loo and emptied her bladder. What had happened, anyway? She retraced her steps in the deli. She'd bought a sandwich and then turned around to try and get out of the narrow space that ran along the counter that served as both an entrance and an exit. The place had only just opened and was full of office workers trying something new in their routine. She'd been lucky to get there when she did; ten minutes later, the queue was almost at the door. With her sandwich and purse both tucked to her chest, she'd smiled awkwardly at the pretty woman in red queuing behind her as they tried to politely manoeuvre around each other without rubbing, which proved a physical impossibility. Eryn wasn't really paying that much attention – she just wanted to get home and take advantage of a rare afternoon off from school. The teacher training day had finished early, which was something of a miracle, and for once she was going to spend it not marking books, but lying on the sofa and catching up with all the telly she'd recorded that Alan didn't like watching.

The unavoidable had happened, and she'd knocked into the slim woman as she squeezed her size fourteen hips through the narrow gap. She'd glanced back to smile an apology at her, but the woman was already giving her order to the overworked young man behind the counter. It was bright in the shop but there'd been an area of darkness on the back of the woman's dress. Where could that shadow have been coming from? Was it a shadow at all? She'd almost reached out to touch it, but then, as if feeling the eyes on her back, the woman had turned and given her a tight smile. Eryn had gone on her way after that. The TV was waiting and the cramped quarters of the deli were irritating. She wouldn't go there again.

She was reaching for the toilet paper, still confused as to why such a mundane sandwich purchase could have woken her up in such a state of fear, when she gasped again, one hand flying to her mouth. It was the woman. The woman and the bank statement. It was all... it was all making sense. She remembered. Oh god, she remembered. Her eyes widened in the gloom.

'No, you don't understand.' She paces around the living room. The house is still her own, but there is no computer console cluttered messily at the base of the TV, and flowers sit in a vase on the window sill and the cushions are pink, not the later pink-and-brown compromise that she will never really like

and is pretty sure Alan doesn't either. Compromise could be funny like that. Ignore things people like and just go for something neither is over-impressed by. They don't tell you that's where it's leading in all the romcoms.

She stares at the young man with the slightly arrogant walk and London accent. Why is he so calm? 'They're not normal children. They have faces behind their faces. I saw it! They'll hurt the other children!'

The man touches his ear and then looks at the tall woman standing in the doorway. 'They're contained. Jack's got the two at the school and Tosh got the two in the house.'

'Any sign of the original family?' The woman – Suzie, she'd said her name was Suzie – asked.

'In the basement. Not very pretty.'

'Are you listening to me at all?' Eryn asks. Who are these people? They aren't the police, even though it's the police she called after what happened the previous evening.

'Don't worry,' the man – Owen – says. 'We've caught them. There won't be any more trouble.'

'But what about Billy Grainger?' Eryn asks. 'Did they hurt little Billy?' The man and the woman look at each other and she sees it all in that glance. Billy Grainger won't be in her class if they ever let her go to school today. Little Billy with his squint and his knees that pointed inwards is done with school. He's done with life. 'Oh no,' she says, and puts one hand over her mouth.

'Come into the kitchen,' Suzie says, resting a

gentle hand on her arm. 'I'll make a pot of tea.'

Eryn allows herself to be led out of the sitting room where the suited man is talking quietly through whatever kind of phone is in his ear, and she sits at the round pine kitchen table that looks so ordinary with her post opened from yesterday still littering it. A gas bill and a bank statement, nothing exciting, there never is, but she was going to file it away when she got home. After everything that's happened, she'd completely forgotten.

'I saw them with Billy in the playground,' she whispers.

Suzie Costello is adding tea bags to the pot and waiting for the kettle to boil. She doesn't turn around.

'I knew something was wrong when I saw that,' Eryn continues. She doesn't know if the woman is listening and she doesn't really care. She just needs to say it again as if maybe by repeating it over and over she can get it out of her system and get back to being sensible Eryn Bunting, a nice young girl, responsible primary teacher, a little old for her time but that's all right because she quite likes being that way. 'Nobody ever plays with Billy. He's the one that even the teachers have a hard time liking.'

She pauses then – she feels bad saying it even though it's true and even though it can hardly hurt Billy now – but it feels wrong. 'But those two little girls were playing with him. They were pretty girls too.' She looks up at the woman. 'Twins. I didn't recognise them, which is strange because I know most of the children in the school, even if only by sight. It's like a sixth sense with teachers, that ability to recognise your own. They had Billy's hands and then they just led him right out of the gate and Billy didn't so much as look back, even though all the children know that they can't go out of the gate at playtime.' She frowns with the memory. 'I banged on the window but they didn't hear me. I could see Anna, who was on gate duty, telling Jimmy Logan off for something and she hadn't seen them.' She can remember every detail perfectly. The classroom smelled of dusty central heating and her heels clattered on the parquet wooden floor of the old building as she ran outside. She banged her hand on the door frame and it really hurt but she didn't stop.

'I called after them,' she says. 'The bell had just gone and all the other children were lining up to come back inside, but I ran out of the gate. They were just going round the corner and into that bit of woody wasteland that people keep saying is going to be nice new flats but has been empty for ages apart from the hoarding. I'm not much of a sprinter and I had heels on – only low ones, but still not exactly running shoes.' She can remember how her legs burned with the sudden exertion and her large breasts bounced painfully under her jumper. She can remember wondering what was scaring her so much. This wasn't a strange man with sweets luring one of her children into a car or something, this was just children sneaking off to play. Still, she couldn't fight the dread that coursed through her veins. Something wasn't right. Not at all. It was those children and they had Billy and they weren't HER children and there was something very wrong because they were playing with Billy and no one ever played with Billy.

'They must have been walking fast, because they were quite far across the muddy ground and were weaving their way through the bushes. I called after them again but they didn't stop until they were sheltered in the middle of a thicket. That's when they finally looked my way.' A sob caught a little in her throat. 'Billy was crying when he turned around. He saw me and he looked so scared. He started to call out and one of them lifted her hand and wrapped it round his mouth. His glasses tilted funny on his face. It was so weird. She looked like she was barely exerting herself, but poor Billy's face was all squashed in her grip.' She looks up and swallows. It's so hard to believe. Just thinking about it now she feels crazy.

'It's over now. A cup of tea and getting it off your chest will make you feel better.' Suzie is getting milk out of the fridge and gives her a half-smile as she speaks. It's sympathetic but Eryn can see she's not really listening. How can all this seem so ordinary to her? And to those others?

'The other one turned round and looked at me. She was so pretty. Maybe 6 or 7. About Billy's age, I suppose, but he's always been smaller than the other kids. She smiled right at me and I stopped moving forward. I don't even know why.' Her nose was running and she wiped it on the back of her hand. 'She was laughing at me. I could tell. I looked behind me, hoping Anna had come too, but there was no one there. I was so scared. Not as scared as Billy, but so scared. I looked at Billy, stuck and so small between them and I could see that he really thought I could help him. That I would just make them let him go. That's what adults do, isn't it?' Suzie puts the mug of tea in front of her and she wraps her hands round it, needing its warmth. 'That's when it happened. The one that smiled at me, she just reached up and tugged at her pony tail. I didn't understand what was happening at first. It looked so odd. And then I saw the skin coming away from her face and showing what was underneath. All those TEETH.' She gasps at the memory. 'Just teeth. Sharp, shiny teeth. Rows and rows of them. It turned my way again and I knew there was nothing I could do but run. It wasn't real. It couldn't be real. That's what I thought. And god help me, as the second one started to pull its face off, I turned and ran all the way back to school.'

She's shivering, and Suzie leans in to steady the mug in her hands before she spills it. 'Drink that. It'll make you feel better.' She has dark serious eyes, but Eryn wonders how anything could make her feel better ever again. She holds the mug but doesn't drink it. She's still lost in the re-living of the previous afternoon. She thinks she will be for ever.

'I ran into my classroom and went to the window. My class were all confused, and the TA was trying to get them organised with art stuff and *was calling to me to help but I ignored them all. I watched the gate as the minutes ticked away. I'd almost convinced myself it had never happened at all and it was all in my head, like some kind of brain tumour making me see things, when the two blonde girls came back to school, holding hands with each other and no sign of Billy. I've never been so scared in all my life. I couldn't stay. I faked a migraine, went home and then called the police.'*

'You did the right thing.' Suzie sips her own tea, and Eryn raises her mug.

'What happened to Billy?' she asks, and then takes a sip. She knows the answer, but she needs to hear it out loud.

'They ate him,' Suzie says, and Eryn starts to cry properly.

'Who are you?' she asks. 'Who are you people?'

'We're Torchwood,' Suzie answers, as if that explains everything. Eryn drinks her tea.

It was all there. Everything. She remembered it. And more. She sat in the gloom of the bathroom, her pants down around her knees still, and her mouth dropped open slightly. Billy wasn't run over. Not like she remembered it. Those girls had eaten him. There were things like that everywhere, she was sure of it, and there was Torchwood to stop them. That's what they did. Torchwood. The young man and the woman. It was the woman that she was thinking about now though. She pushed the image of long-dead Billy to one side. She couldn't help him then, and she couldn't help him now.

It was the woman. The woman in the deli. Suzie Costello.

One hand rose to her mouth and her brain itched like crazy as the pieces came together. She'd sat at her kitchen table and drunk tea with Suzie Costello, and then she'd forgotten everything. She'd fallen asleep. When she'd woken up she was hazy. Not quite ill but not quite well either. She took a couple of days off work and that's when she found out that Billy had been knocked down and killed, and then she'd been upset and little things like that month's filing went out of her head. But now she remembered – it was clear as a bell in her head. The bank statement was on her kitchen table when Suzie Costello made the tea that made her forget. But after that, it wasn't there. She could see the gas bill but not the bank statement.

Suzie Costello had taken it. She knew that, just as she knew that Suzie Costello was the woman she'd bumped into at the deli, the woman with the dark shadow on her back. She trembled in the gloom and hot tears spilled down her cold cheeks. She remembered everything. Torchwood. Torchwood were meant to *protect* them from things like the girls that ate Billy, that's what they did, but now Suzie Costello had the darkness inside her, the terrible, terrible darkness that was so hungry and wanted to play with them and make them scream and never let them die and…

Eryn got up from the toilet, pulled up her knickers with trembling hands and then locked the door. She was freezing, and her legs numb from sitting half naked for so long. How long? She didn't know. She didn't care. Suzie Costello had the darkness inside her – she'd seen it on her back. And now that she'd seen it, it would come for her, she knew that, and the darkness would be far worse than the thing with the teeth that had eaten poor Billy. The darkness was everything in every nightmare she'd ever had.

There was a lipstick in the bathroom cabinet and she wrote her message with it on the bathroom wall.

I REMEMBER.

Eryn Bunting was as sensible and practical in her death as she was in her life. She smashed the glass of the cabinet mirror and sliced her wrists open with two deft slices, straight up the vein, not across. She sat on the toilet again and let out a sigh. The glass breaking wouldn't have woken Alan. He'd stretched out across her side of the bed and would be sleeping like a baby. Black spots appeared in the corner of her vision. Not her side of the bed any more. She didn't mind the nothing that crept in and stole her away. Nothing lived in it. Nothing that would make her scream.

Chapter Twenty-Three

Suzie let the chemistry take hold. For the first five minutes or so in the cab, they'd kept themselves under control, but as soon as the driver had turned off the main road and the back of the car was in relative seclusion, she and the policeman were all over each other. They just couldn't help themselves.

By the time they tumbled through the door to his small flat, they were laughing and tearing at each other's clothes, kicking their shoes off as he half-carried her into the bedroom.

'Excuse the mess,' he muttered, shoving abandoned shirts and trousers to one side so they could fall onto the unmade bed. She giggled as his knee caught awkwardly on her skirt and he laughed back before kissing her some more. A rush of warmth overwhelmed her. This wasn't like it had been the night before with the stranger whose dead mess now littered her own apartment. This was *normal*. She liked him. She really did. She hadn't felt like this in such a long time, even before she'd spent such a long time dead. This was old Suzie back, girly and soft and just wanting him to sweep her up in his arms and make everything OK.

Their breathing got heavier and she felt the yawning space inside her opening up. The shadows that surrounded her were reaching for him but she pulled them back, containing it all inside. The darkness couldn't leak out; not here, not now. *No*, she thought. *No, you can't have him.* She closed her eyes. *Not yet. Not ever.*

His mouth was warm on her neck. She had to kill him, she knew that, and she would, she really would, when this was done, but she wouldn't give him to the place on the other side of the gateway she had become. She wouldn't let the darkness have him. She closed herself off to everything but his touch.

Afterwards, when they were finished, she dozed off, content on his chest. Killing could wait. Everything could wait. Just for a little while.

Sirens wailed through the Cardiff night as the shadows stretched across the city. The black patches left in the woman's wake expanded hungrily. She was distracted and it could play. It needed MORE. There was so much pain to explore. It was becoming impatient with her containing it. Soon it would be too strong for her and it would pour out through her eyes and consume them all, but for now it stretched as far as it could in the patches that had leaked from her.

On his way home from the theatre, Colin

Friend was wondering at the unfairness of his life. He was a good actor, but never quite good enough it would seem. Slightly too short for this role, not quite handsome enough for that and not quite ugly enough for the staple diet of 'character' parts. He was nearly 40 and living in a studio flat in bloody Wales for the duration of the run – which after tonight's poor audience showing might not be anywhere near as long as planned – and had actually been grateful to get the gig in the first place.

When he'd left drama school, he'd been so full of high expectations but, as much as he tried to keep the dream alive, now that his hairline was receding and the offers of work were thinning just as quickly, it was hard to keep the bitterness at bay. He lit a pre-rolled cigarette – no Marlboro Lights on his pay cheque – and inhaled hard. What would he do if he gave up acting anyway? He wasn't qualified for anything else. At some point, though, he was going to have to make financial plans or he was going to end up back in his mum's spare bedroom, and that was something he could live without.

As it turned out, money was no longer going to be a worry for Colin Friend. Nor in fact were the terrible reviews that would hit the local papers the next day calling his performance 'the worst Macbeth in the history of the Scottish play', one saying he 'didn't know whether to laugh or cry and neither in a good way'. These things were soon to be completely insignificant to Colin, who, as he rounded the final corner to the slightly tired modern block he was renting in, spotted a strange dark shadow against the bus shelter.

He wouldn't have stopped at all if the cat, only its front paws and head visible, hadn't yowled. It was an awful sound, not the normal angry hiss associated with the independent animal, but a cry of pain and terror. Colin liked cats. His mum had two, and sometimes he thought he liked those old moggies more than he liked her. He wondered if the cat was trapped or stuck to something, or maybe had been hit by a car and knocked into the gloom and, throwing his cigarette away, he trotted over to it.

He frowned as he crouched down and stroked the cat's head. Its ears were pressed flat against its head and it was trembling. Nothing was visible from the midsection, and its lower body was lost in the pitch-black shadow falling across the back of the bus shelter. The oddness of the dark was forgotten.

'Let's get you out of there and take a look,' Colin said softly. As last words go, they weren't the ones he'd planned to send into posterity, but then neither was this exactly how he'd envisaged his last moments in this dimension. There would be no wailing fans. There wouldn't even be a body. His hand reached into the shadow and then he froze. What the…?

Within moments, both the man and the cat were gone, and if there had been anyone passing to listen, they might just have heard the very faintest of terrible screams.

It would be a small comfort to Colin Friend, if there were any comfort left in his tortured eternal existence, to know that he wasn't alone. Over the course of the night, fifteen more people stepped into unusual black patches. One stumbled out of one dimension and into the next while drunk, the others were simply victims of their own curiosity. One was the Mayor's driver, who'd had to wait so long for his boss that he ended up stopping on the way home to take a piss up against a wall and thought the dark shadow would hide him from view. It certainly did that. He arrived in Hell with his flies undone.

In other parts of town, several people committed suicide after scrawling 'I Remember' somewhere it could be seen. The message wasn't for anyone in particular, it just needed to be out. Torchwood and the terrible blackness had become one for them, and with Torchwood gone, there was only the blackness left and they knew, although the rest of the city hadn't woken up to it, that the blackness was coming. It would swallow the people and then the city and then the entire world and there was no one left to stop it.

It was coming. The screaming of millions.

When Suzie woke up, she was still tired and incredibly bleary, confusion coming from inside her. It was as if she was both in the room and also spread across the city at the same time. Her ears ached as if someone had shrieked right into them.

It was the strangest sensation and she shivered slightly. What had happened? Had the world inside her escaped a little while she'd drifted? She felt the darkness pull back inside, curled up and secure behind her eyes. Maybe it was just that sleep had eluded her since her most recent resurrection and now that she'd finally dozed off her body wanted more. For the first time, she hoped that was so.

The sheets smelled of washing powder and cotton and for the first time in a long time, she felt something close to normal. It couldn't last of course, she knew that, but she wanted to enjoy it before the morning rolled around and she'd have to kill him and disappear into her strange new life. She stretched one arm out. She didn't want to kill him yet. *She didn't want to kill him ever.* She squashed the old Suzie's thought, but she couldn't quite squash the feeling that came with it. There was something about Tom Cutler that stopped her feeling lonely. No one else had ever done that. She had an awful precognition that when she killed him she'd be lonely for ever. Her hand found nothing and she sat up on one elbow and looked around. He wasn't in the room.

She found him in the lounge. The curtains were open wide and he was by the window, sitting on the edge of an armchair and staring out at the night. He lit one cigarette with the butt of another.

'What is it?' she mumbled, tying his tatty dressing gown around her waist.

'I remember,' he said, softly. 'I woke up and

remembered everything.'

'What?'

'Torchwood.' He turned to look at her. 'I remember Torchwood.'

For a moment Suzie froze, her eyes darting cautiously around the room for something to attack him with should he lunge at her, adrenalin surging through her still body, and the darkness forming a sudden cloud behind her eyes, but then he turned back to the window and drew in a long lungful of smoke.

'You might want to sit down because this is going to sound crazy,' he said. 'They were a special unit. Dealt with aliens and alien technology. The first time my path crossed with theirs was in London. The details of the case don't really matter, what matters is the whole thing messed me up. There was an alien inside a man – making him do things. I *saw* it. I'd been so keen to take him down and then when I saw what I did – impossible as it was – I couldn't. Torchwood came and dealt with the alien, but they sure as shit weren't as good with the human fallout. I had to manage that. I screwed up my career over it. Couldn't let an innocent man go to prison, no matter what they said. I said I'd planted evidence and the judge threw the case out.' He shook his head. 'Jesus.'

Torchwood One. Suzie felt her panic ease slightly. It was Torchwood One he was talking about. If she was careful she might be OK here. She needed to react like a normal person would. Like she'd seen so many times in the old days.

'Aliens?' she said, softly. 'You mean like illegal ones from other countries?'

'No.' He laughed a little. 'I mean like the real deal. Outer space. Bloody Torchwood. I got transferred down here after that, my glittering career over. And then along came the opera murders. Until tonight,' he gazed down at the glowing end of his cigarette, 'that whole case was in my memory exactly like it was reported in the papers. One man gone mad. Practising on others and then murdering his wife to pay off their debts. But it wasn't like that at all. Not really. I remember standing out in the rain when we found the first body all opened up in the church and with its voicebox missing, and then, lo and behold, they turned up again. A different team, but Torchwood all the same. Captain Jack Harkness and that pretty little ex-copper and the Welsh coffee lover. I knew as soon as they stepped out of that SUV that it was going to be all the weird shit all over again and I was going to end up more screwed up than I had been the first time round. And I was right. We got the alien, though. That time it worked out all OK. They were good people, those three. When it was over, we went to a bar, I had a beer with Jack and then,' his eyes narrowed slightly, 'nothing. Everything was forgotten.'

'Aliens?' she coughed out a small laugh. 'In Cardiff? Did someone put something in your champagne?'

'No,' Cutler said, softly. 'But Captain Jack Harkness put something in my beer I think.' He smiled at her. 'Come here.'

Suzie stood between his legs and he pulled her down so that she too was seated on the edge of the armchair with him behind her. He wrapped one arm around her waist and even in this cautious situation she couldn't fight that it felt good. She belonged with him. This sudden revelation, unsettling as it was, confirmed it to her. They'd both been messed up by Torchwood and Captain Jack Harkness. If they were damaged souls, then it was that immortal man's fault. She leaned her head back on Cutler shoulder. 'Nothing as exciting as aliens comes to Wales.'

'Look up there.' Cutler pointed one finger up to the night sky. His breath was warm against her neck and she wanted to smile. Here with him, she was as close to happy as she'd ever been. Maybe she could persuade him to come with her. Maybe if she could just explain... the thought drifted away. How could she possibly explain what she'd done?

'What?' she said, her voice light.

'Somewhere up there in space is a rift. Some kind of cut in space or something, and all manner of shit comes through it. Including aliens.'

'Over Cardiff?'

'Yes.'

'So where are these people now?' she asked. 'This Torchwood?'

'I don't know where they are, but here's the funny part. The site you're working on? That Commander Jackson is excavating?'

'What about it?'

'That was their base. The Hub, they called it. There was a lift where the water tower used to be. If you came out that way then no one in the street could see you until you stepped off. What a crazy place. Jackson and his people must be trying to get out as much of the alien shit stored there as they can.' He leaned sideways and lit another cigarette, blowing the smoke away from her body. 'I bet there'll be something alien at the bottom of these murders too. No wonder I've been drawn to the site all this time. My brain has been trying to make me remember.'

'The site? Where I'm working?' She thought carefully before speaking. She couldn't overplay this. 'God, I'd heard rumours that it was something a little bit *X Files*, but alien hunters? It's too much to take in.'

'Have a dig around in your boss's computer tomorrow. Or sneak a peek at the stuff they're bringing out. Then you'll believe me. There's been enough weird shit going on if you think about it. When all the kids went freaky for one.'

'Yes,' Suzie said. 'The more I think about it, the more I can see it. They're definitely bringing some strange stuff out of the wreckage of that building, and I suppose that's why they have Department scientists there. Like the one who died.'

'There's something else,' Cutler said. 'I've got this bad feeling. A really bad feeling. Like something terrible is coming, and there's nothing I can do to stop it. It's like a doorway's been opened somewhere and it needs to be closed.'

Suzie turned to face him and cupped his face in her hands. 'You've had a shock, that's all. This sudden rush of memories is bound to be unsettling. Let's go back to bed and get a couple of hours' sleep and then come to work with me. We can talk to the boss. See what he's got to say.'

'I remember,' Cutler muttered, looking at some empty space over her shoulder. 'That's what the suicides wrote. The same two words that are ringing in my head.'

'What suicides?' Suzie asked.

'They remembered.' Cutler was momentarily lost in his own thoughts. 'Just like me. These people – I think they were given the same drug I was. Whatever it was that made us all forget. And now they're remembering.'

Retcon. That's what they would have given him. 'But you don't feel like killing yourself, do you?' she asked. Despite herself, her curiosity was engaged, just as it would have been back when she was Torchwood. She was pretty much all that was left of Torchwood now. The last one standing. You could never keep a good girl down. Not even with a couple of stints of death.

'No.' Cutler shook his head and then stroked her hair out of her face, tucking it carefully behind one of her ears. 'Certainly not tonight. I feel a bit like my whole life of late has been a lie, but I don't feel suicidal.' He pulled her mouth towards his and kissed her. 'Quite far from it,' he continued when they broke away, 'even with this sense that something bad is coming.'

'So why would these people kill themselves and not you?'

'I don't know. Maybe because I'd already had an experience with Torchwood in London before the Cardiff lot gave me their drugs? I knew about Torchwood and all this alien stuff for *years* before they wiped me. These people might have been only a day or so. Perhaps that's the difference. What if this feeling of dread is worse for them somehow? Maybe we're remembering because we *have* to. Because this is some kind of alien thing that's coming – something so terrible that our basic survival instinct is kicking in and because we've come across this stuff before we can *see* it in a way ordinary people can't?'

'That's a lot of maybes,' Suzie said. A haggard, haunted look had settled on Cutler and she found it suited him better than his previous almost carefree expression. Jack Harkness had been stupid not to hire DI Tom Cutler. He'd have been better than Miss sweet-and-sickly Gwen bloody Cooper. Maybe Jack was incapable of hiring someone that didn't want to sleep with him. She swallowed the bile. Torchwood was gone. Maybe she and Cutler could start their own branch... maybe they could go somewhere like America...

She shut the thoughts down. There was no future for them. It was a childish idea that belonged to the old Suzie who, somewhere deep down, just wanted everything to be normal again. That Suzie was dead, she reminded herself. If she hadn't been totally eradicated the first time round, the second long stretch of nothing had finished her off.

She couldn't let Cutler live. He was too smart. Soon enough he'd figure out that she *was* the bad thing that was coming. It was all inside her on the other side of her eyes.

'Let's go back to bed,' she said, gently. 'There's nothing we can do about it all now. In a couple of hours it will be morning, and then we'll find the Commander. I promise.' She leaned forward and kissed his head. 'I'll get you a glass of water.' She smiled. 'For after.'

Her eyes watered as she wrapped herself around him again and she swallowed down the tears. They still had an hour or two before she'd have to kill him and she wanted to make the most of it.

Chapter Twenty-Four

When Cutler woke up, he was struck by three things. First, that his head felt as if a truck had driven through it, second that his phone was ringing, and third, that the space beside him in the bed was empty. He frowned and peeled his tongue from the roof of his mouth. God, he felt like crap.

'Sue?' he called out, his voice like gravel. There was no answer. The flat was silent, no running water from the shower, nor a kettle boiling in the kitchen. He sat up, ignoring the throbbing drumbeat in his skull and looking around the room. Her clothes were gone. What time was it? Somewhere on the floor his phone stopped ringing, which came as a momentary relief, and he rolled over to grab his watch. It was gone eight o'clock and he swore under his breath as he kicked the covers off and tumbled out. Why hadn't she woken him up?

His head spun slightly, and he stumbled as he headed to the bathroom. If he didn't know better he'd think he had a hangover, but he hadn't drunk enough and he'd been fine before they went to sleep. He glanced at the half-drunk glass of water by the bed. Had she slipped him a sleeping pill? His head felt drugged, he couldn't deny that, but why would she? Did she want to speak to Commander Jackson without any interference from him? Maybe this fuzziness was just fallout from what he'd remembered. As he brushed his teeth, a familiar stranger stared back. This Tom Cutler didn't go running in the mornings and get early nights and always stop after two or three beers. This was the one who smoked for breakfast and last thing at night, and felt the urge to trip up smug joggers if they happened to cross his path. Overnight, dark circles had formed under his eyes to welcome him back, and he splashed water over his face and body to shake the mugginess away, then ran his fingers through his hair. He needed a shower – after last night he definitely needed a shower – but he didn't have time. He sprayed a coating of deodorant over his skin and headed back into his bedroom. His mobile started ringing again as he grabbed his shirt from the previous evening and pulled it on. He'd only worn it for a few hours and it would have to do.

'I know I'm late,' he muttered into the phone while lighting a cigarette. 'I'll be there...'

'... as soon as you can, I hope,' Andy Davidson finished his sentence for him. 'We've got three more suicides reported, and I doubt that's it. We're getting loads of missing people being reported too. I don't know what the hell happened last night, but something's freaking Cardiff out.'

A wave of terror and foreboding rushed through Cutler's system, the sudden adrenalin rush that came with it killing off his headache. He sucked hard on his cigarette. 'Give me ten minutes.'

He tried Sue's number on the way to the car but it rang out. Maybe she kept it in her bag while she was working. The answerphone kicked in and he listened to the mechanical message, slightly sad not to hear her voice. 'Hey, it's me,' he said. 'Look, thanks for letting me sleep in, but I'm going to head over to the site when I've checked in at the station. Don't do anything until I get there. I don't want you to get into trouble, OK?' He paused and then hung up, not sure how to say goodbye. He'd probably see her before she heard it anyway.

The drive through the rush-hour traffic did little to clear his thinking, nor shake his sense of unease, and when he got to work, the first thing he wanted was to make sure that he wasn't going crazy and that these were real memories that had come back to him so suddenly. Bypassing Andy Davidson who was signalling to him while on a desk phone, Cutler strode into his boss's office.

'Knocking is the polite way to get my attention, Cutler,' DCI Waterman said, looking up from his desk.

'Torchwood,' Cutler said. He saw the defensive tension immediately tighten up in Waterman's shoulders. Bingo. 'You've heard of them, then?'

'Not for a while. Don't ask me for details because

I don't have any. They weren't in my remit.'

'Did they step in and take over some cases?' he asked.

'Sometimes.' Waterman leaned back, his lips pursed. 'Why?'

'Did they help out on the opera singer case? My big case?'

'Are you saying you don't remember?'

'Humour me.' Cutler knew the answer. He'd known it as soon as his boss had reacted to the mention of Torchwood, but he needed to hear it. It was as if a film was being peeled away from the world and he was seeing it clearly.

'They might have done. You worked the case, but they had an interest. What the hell is all this about?'

Cutler was saved answering by Andy Davidson opening the door.

'Doesn't anyone knock any more?' Waterman asked.

'Sorry, sir.' Andy looked at Cutler. 'You're not going to believe this. The suicide count is now at seven, and one of the names that came up was Eryn Bunting.'

'The teacher? The one whose bank statement was taken to open the safety deposit box?' Cutler gave a short nod to their bemused DCI who was shooing them away, and walked out of his office with the sergeant. 'Are you sure it's her?'

'Yes. She slashed her wrists in the bathroom and wrote "I remember" on the wall.'

Cutler's mind reeled. If his theory about the

suicides was right, that meant Eryn Bunting's memory had been wiped by Torchwood at some point. If Sue's story was true, then the murders started at the Hub, and something was taken out of a safety deposit box set up years ago in Eryn Bunting's name. Did someone steal her bank statement while her memory was being wiped? Surely only someone in this elusive Torchwood team could have done that.

Torchwood. *Everything* was Torchwood, and Torchwood was *everything*. The dread that was growing inside him, that was Torchwood too. He knew it in every fibre of his being. Torchwood had been woven into his life for ever, it seemed, and destroyed as the Hub might be, it wasn't letting go yet. What the hell was going on? He needed to get to the site and talk to the Commander. Something bigger than murder was going on here.

Screaming. The screaming of millions. He didn't understand the sudden thought and, wrapped around the dread as it was, he pushed it to one side. He didn't have time for a terror he couldn't explain. Not until he'd got to the bottom of this. Something else was bugging him. Something Sue had said to him the previous night had set an alarm bell ringing in his head and he couldn't put his finger on what it was.

'I want to know about Bunting's background,' he said to Andy. 'Get in touch with her school. Let me know if there was anything strange or out of the ordinary that happened around the time her bank statement went missing.'

'Why?'

'I'll let you know if it comes to anything.' He was sending the sergeant to do an unnecessary job, but he wanted to handle this on his own. Torchwood had messed up his life – he wasn't going to let it get the young sergeant too. Whatever was going on here, he'd figure it out himself. He shut the door to his office and dialled Jackson's office. He hoped that Sue Costa would answer but instead the Commander barked a greeting into his ear.

'I need to come in and talk to you,' Cutler said. 'It's urgent. I'll be there as soon as I can. Don't go anywhere.' He let the Commander start his protests before he cut him off. 'These murders are wrapped up with Torchwood, and since you're sitting on the Hub I need answers from you.' He hung up before they could get into a conversation. This was something they needed to do face to face, and the Commander could sweat for a bit. He'd almost got to the end of the Incident Room when a young constable called him back. She looked flushed and excited.

'It's the tech team, sir,' she said. 'That CCTV you wanted? From the first two suicide locations? They've been through it all and they've got something.'

Cutler stared at her. Commander Jackson was going to have to wait another half an hour.

Chapter Twenty-Five

Elwood Jackson stayed on the phone for a moment or two after the policeman had hung up, the empty tone doing little to ease his sudden anxiety. How the hell did Cutler know about the Hub? It was true that some of the police – especially the Cardiff police – knew of Torchwood's existence, but not in any detail, and they certainly didn't know about the Hub. What had changed? What the hell had Cutler found out about these murders that had brought him that information?

He rubbed his forehead and sighed. It was first thing in the morning and he was tired already. The Department weren't going to be happy about this, but what the hell was he supposed to do about it? He'd never been a great sleeper but over the past few nights the hours he'd got had dwindled below five and were filled with nightmares of being terrified and trapped in Hell. They disturbed him, mainly because he wasn't a man with much imagination and the creatures that loomed out of the darkness in these dreams were beyond anything he thought his mind could make up.

On top of that, with the deaths and mutilations he'd seen on various battlefields over the years, he hadn't thought Hell could hold anything that might frighten him. If the experiences in his sleep were anything to go by, then he'd thought wrong.

He almost jumped when the phone on the desk rang again, and he answered it gruffly. If it was the policeman with any more snappy demands, he had a good mind to tell him to go and shove his cockiness where the sun didn't shine. It wasn't Cutler, however, but the Department records administrator.

'You put in a request about a deleted file, sir?' she said.

'Yes, that's right. Have you got the information for me?'

'Yes.' The woman paused at the other end. 'You wanted to know who deleted it and when?'

'That's right.' His patience, thin as it was that morning, was disappearing. 'I haven't got all day.'

'It's just that...' She hesitated. 'It's just that, according to the system, *you* deleted it. Yesterday morning.'

'What?' Jackson froze. 'What do you mean, *I* deleted it?'

'It was deleted with your clearance. All back-up files. I can't even tell you whose file it was – not without going down and searching through the paper files for a match and that will take days.'

'Do it,' he grunted.

'But sir, I...'

Commander Elwood Jackson hung up. His heart raced and, as it thumped, the start of a headache beat out a rhythm in time with it in his skull. If he wasn't careful he'd be heading for a stroke or an aneurism or something equally unpleasant. He didn't understand this situation at all. He hadn't deleted the file, so the only other possibility was that someone else had compromised his computer. But who? Who was this person who had managed to delete all trace of themselves in the system? Most soldiers and Department men had their DNA logged in several databases. If they hadn't found their man in their own files they'd normally come up somewhere else.

He was starting to actually look forward to Cutler's arrival. Maybe if he and the policeman shared their information they might both come up with some answers instead of both drowning in questions. He needed some coffee and stared at the empty machine. Where the hell was Sue Costa? Surely she should be here by now? How late had she stayed at the party? She didn't strike him as the kind of girl to get too drunk and sleep in late. She was too efficient for that. He'd give it ten minutes and then call her – it looked like he was going to have to make the coffee himself.

He'd set the machine gurgling and was waiting impatiently for the jug to fill when Lt Howe knocked on the door and came in. Jackson expected to see the policeman behind him, but he was alone. He almost asked him to find out who'd been in the Portakabin when he'd been out the previous day, but then decided against it. He'd wait and hear what Cutler had to say first. The last thing he needed was gossip amongst the men. The Department would no doubt be firing him for incompetence soon enough without him making it worse.

'Lieutenant?' he said.

'It's one of the pieces of equipment we've retrieved, sir. Not alien, but human. The handheld monitor?'

'Go on.'

'The tech team have got it working again. The specifications for it were stored in the back-up drive.'

'Get to the point, soldier.' The machine finished bubbling and Jackson poured himself a mug, glad that his hand was steady. He had a feeling that in a moment he was going to need something stronger, but coffee was going to have to do for now.

'We're picking up some very unusual readings from it. Massive spikes in activity. We're trying to pinpoint the focus and locations, but we're learning as we go.'

'Could it just be faulty or damaged?' Jackson asked.

'No, sir. As far as we can tell, the machine is working perfectly. We just need to understand what it's trying to tell us.'

'Then get back to it, and I want to know the minute you have anything further.' The Rift Monitor. That's what Howe was talking about. If the handheld one was showing lots of activity then there was something alien at work in Cardiff.

'Yes, sir.' Howe disappeared and, as the door closed behind him, Commander Jackson sipped his coffee. God, it was awful. He never quite got the quantities right. Where the hell was Sue Costa?

Chapter Twenty-Six

Suzie sat in the train station and listened once again to Tom Cutler's message on her phone. Around her, people scurried on their way to this train or that, eyes fixed on departure boards or looking for waiting friends rather than the dark shadows that crept too far from her body to be quite natural. No one sat in the seats around her, though, and despite her hunched shoulders and the tears streaming down her face, not a single stranger stopped to check on the beautiful crying woman in the middle of the station. Their sixth sense was working quietly for them by ignoring her. Those that walked by might not think they'd noticed her sitting so still in the midst of the hubbub, but their dreams that night would be plagued by darkness and demons and pain.

Suzie felt alone. She was also terrified. She should have killed Tom Cutler. She really should have. Why hadn't she? It couldn't be love, that would just be ridiculous. It had to be the bond she felt with him over Torchwood. Something about that shared experience made her vulnerable to him. He'd *weakened* her. Her eyes blurred with fresh tears and she clenched her fists with frustration at herself. It was all going wrong – she could feel it. The darkness was too greedy, and although she'd killed another two since leaving the policeman's flat it wanted *more*. It was always going to want so much more. She was coming to realise that it wanted it all. It wanted to take the whole world into its black embrace and drag it through her to the place between dimensions and she had no idea at all how to stop it, and even if she could.

Her best chance was to spend her life feeding it and hope that it would die with her when the nothing eventually came for her again. Somewhere in the last twenty-four hours, that future had started to feel a little like hell. That moment had come at precisely the point when she'd realised that she couldn't kill stupid DI Tom Cutler, because the old Suzie, the one that she'd thought was dead but it seemed was very much alive, had gone and felt sorry for Cutler. He'd been messed up enough. She felt connected to him in a way she hadn't with anyone else. Bloody Torchwood had made wrecks of them both. God, she'd been pathetic standing over the bed with the knife. She'd even shoved a sleeping pill into his glass of water so he might feel it less. It hadn't helped. She still couldn't kill him. He looked so calm and handsome lying there asleep, and she couldn't imagine him cold and blue and lost into nothing. It made her cry. And here she was, hours later. Still crying.

She looked up at the board again. Any one of those trains would do for now. She needed to get to London, get to her secondary safety deposit box in the basement of Selfridges, and then catch a flight to somewhere warm. They'd never catch her, not if she kept new Suzie in charge. She was too clever for them. Cutler might, though. He'd want answers. Especially when he *knew* about her. What scared her most was that she almost liked the idea of him catching her. It would mean she could get to *see* him again. For the first time in what seemed like forever, she wished Jack Harkness was here. Perhaps he could make things right. Maybe he could get rid of the screaming that was starting to fill her head.

She looked back up at the board but, as the creeping shadows lengthened a little on either side of her, she still couldn't bring herself to move.

'Play it again.' Tom Cutler couldn't believe what he was seeing. A cool slick nausea had crept outwards from his stomach and his face tingled. How could that be? Of all the things that he might have expected to see on the CCTV footage, it wasn't Sue Costa. But there she was. The first film started again and there she was, about to turn down Rebecca Devlin's street, striding confidently in the early morning light, her gaze straight ahead.

'This would be pretty much the time Rebecca Devlin was putting the rubbish out,' Andy Davidson said. 'It's likely they would have seen each other.'

'Play the next clips again.' Cutler's mouth felt like sandpaper. Sue. Sue Costa, if that even was her name, which he now very much doubted. She wasn't answering her phone and had left him sleeping and now this. He thought about the awful vagueness and headache he'd woken up with. Had she drugged him? On screen, she walked out of Andrew Murray's block of flats, and then a second clip played, recorded a few seconds earlier, inside the building. Andrew Murray came in and then pressed the lift button. He yawned but didn't look in any way anxious or unsettled. He didn't twitch or move from foot to foot, but simply stood there, bored, and waited for the lift. Not what anyone would expect from a man half an hour or so away from hanging himself from the balcony.

On the small screen, the lift doors silently opened, and there she was again, Sue Costa, stepping out. They nearly bumped into each other and smiled politely as they passed to counter the awkward moment.

'It's strange,' Andy was leaning so far forward his face almost touched the screen. 'She doesn't speak to him, and neither of them is acting like they know each other. She doesn't even glance back. Surely if she thought she recognised him, she'd turn around?'

'Maybe she doesn't,' he muttered. 'And maybe he didn't remember her until he got upstairs.'

Maybe it wasn't her that Andrew Murray and Rebecca Devlin remembered. He thought about what had happened to him the previous night.

He'd slept with Sue and then all his memories had come back. What was it about her that did that? She wasn't part of Torchwood. He'd never met her before, he was pretty sure about that. But it was Torchwood he remembered, and now she was working at the Hub site, and people were dying and others were killing themselves.

He looked down at his shirt and scanned it closely until he found what he wanted. One long curly hair was stuck to the cotton from where she'd rested her head on his shoulder last night. He pulled it free and handed it to his sergeant. 'Get this over to the lab straight away. I want to know if it matches the samples found on the victims.'

'What? What are you on about?' Andy frowned as he took the hair carefully and held it between his thumb and forefinger. 'Whose is it?'

'Just do it.' Cutler headed for the door. 'And get on to Andrew Murray's block of flats. Get a list of all the residents. What was she doing there? Does she live there or was she visiting someone? A boyfriend, maybe.' Even after everything he'd just learned, that thought made his stomach twist. Was that why she'd wanted to come to his the previous night? Because she lived with someone? It didn't feel true in his heart. Whatever else was going on here, what had happened between them was real. Either that or he was the world's biggest fool.

'Where are you going?' Andy called after him, his confusion clear.

'To get some answers.'

Chapter Twenty-Seven

He'd tried Sue's number four times on the way over to the site, but there was still no answer. Each time it went to her message service, his heart sank. Why wouldn't she talk to him? If she could trust anyone it was him. Whatever mess this was, surely there was a way out of it for them – he couldn't believe that she was a cold-hearted killer. Could he have been that fooled by her? Or could she have felt the same way as he did, regardless of anything else she might have done?

It came as no surprise that she wasn't at the site, and he didn't even glance over at her desk as he strode into the Portakabin.

'It's all linked,' he said. 'The murders. Torchwood. And the suicides.'

'Suicides?' Commander Jackson was on his feet, the desk between them. 'What the hell are you talking about?'

'It's on the news. Along with all kinds of other madness. People missing. People killing themselves. And it's all down to this place.'

'I don't understand. Explain.' Jackson looked

dog-tired, and Cutler took a deep breath before he started. The old man had a lot to take in. Military campaigning and taking orders was one thing, this was a whole heap of other shit.

'Eryn Bunting, the woman whose ID was stolen to open the safety deposit box back in 2007, killed herself last night. She wrote "I remember" on the bathroom wall. There's been a few of those over the past few days. We weren't sure how they were connected, but now I think that all these people killing themselves are remembering their encounters with the Torchwood team. They were given something to make them forget. Some kind of drug. But now their memories are back.' He felt the terror that had been sitting in the pit of his stomach since the previous night. 'And something is scaring them so badly they'd rather die than face it.

'I think whoever took her ID was a member of the Torchwood team and they used the safety deposit box to store something in case of emergencies.'

'How the hell do you know all this about Torchwood? That's confidential. On the phone, you said that this site was the Hub. You *can't* have known that.'

'I've been here before.' Cutler smiled softly. 'I'd just forgotten about it.'

'Jesus.' Commander Jackson sat down.

'The thing that confused me was that I didn't remember *her*. But that doesn't mean she wasn't part of Torchwood. She just wasn't when I met them.'

'You're not making any sense. Who?'

Cutler's phone rang, and he looked down to see Andy Davidson's name glowing on the display. The lab would have been quick – they didn't need to ID the hair, just see whether it matched the ones they already had from the victims. His heart pounded even as his gut told him that he already knew the answer. He'd remembered what it was she said that had been bugging him.

'It's a match,' Andy said. 'Now are you going to tell me what's going on?'

'Call the station and get me the info on that block of flats.'

'But—'

Cutler hung up and stared at the Commander as his heart and stomach raced to his mouth. 'I think you'd better call the Department about Sue Costa.'

'Sue? What about her?' As he spoke, the Commander's eyes widened with the realisation of what Cutler was saying. 'You think she... Dear God.' He sat back heavily in his chair.

'Her hair's a match with those found on the victims. Also she told me something last night. About the *first* victim. The man that died in the vault. The one you neglected to mention?'

Jackson opened his mouth to speak, but Cutler held a hand up to stop him. 'Don't worry about it. That's how you lot operate. The thing is, she told me that he had lovely eyes. She couldn't have known. She arrived here after that murder and the eyes are hardly lovely when they've exploded.'

'There's more,' Jackson said. 'Someone deleted that file from here. From my computer. It must have been her.'

'She's been busy.' Cutler tried to keep the bitterness out of his voice. His heart ached. He'd liked her. He'd *really* liked her. He still did. 'But whatever she's doing to these people, it isn't natural. It must be something alien she's using. Some piece of technology stolen from here. Maybe that's how she killed your first man. She got in somehow, and he came across her and the device killed him.'

'*She* killed him,' Jackson said.

'Sir?' A young man appeared in the doorway. 'These were just emailed over for you. I've printed them out.' He passed an envelope to the Commander and then vanished, not even acknowledging Cutler's presence. Maybe civilians didn't exist to the Army or the Department. They lived in a world of knowledge and secrets, while the rest of the population just bumbled along, just like he'd been doing since Jack Harkness had wiped his memory. Why would anyone take an interest in a world that was oblivious? Why care about the sheep? Thinking of the suicides and the missing people and those unlucky enough to have been caught in Sue Costa's wake, Tom Cutler found that he, unlike the soldiers, cared very much about the ordinary people going about their normal lives. Protecting them was his job, and he intended to do it – even if it meant going after a woman he'd half fallen in some kind of love with.

Jackson was staring down at the contents of the envelope, his mouth half-open. 'You're not going to believe this,' he said eventually.

'Oh, I think I've seen everything.'

'Not this.' Jackson handed over the papers and Cutler stared down at them. He frowned, stuck in disbelief for a moment. 'But this has to be a mistake. This can't...' His voice trailed off as he stared at the picture of Sue Costa – *Suzie Costello*, according to the file – with the word 'DECEASED' stamped across it. 'How can she be dead? This must be a mistake. She must have faked it.'

'Look at the second page. It's Jack Harkness's report on her. Not only is she dead, she's been dead twice.'

Cutler did as the Commander told him. He had to read it twice to take it all in. With the details laid out in black and white as they were, it was hard to see any trace of the woman he'd held in his arms the previous night with her sparkling eyes, soft skin and gentle smile. According to the file, Suzie was a murderer several times over, had tried to kill Gwen Cooper in order to steal her life force. He stared at the last detail. While escaping from Torchwood last time, Suzie had gone to hospital to kill her dying father. Maybe if she hadn't done that, he thought, she might have got away. What had her father done to her that she wanted such a terrible revenge? He stared at the paper and its tale of blood, murder and suicide. He should have felt shocked and appalled – and on a lot of levels he did – but he also pitied her. He knew how

Torchwood could affect your life. What had it done to Suzie Costello?

'She's clearly brilliant,' Jackson said. 'Everything must have been so carefully planned. The first set of back-ups after she shot herself. And now all of this.' He sighed. 'Brilliant and a touch of paranoia.'

'It's only paranoia if it's not true.' Cutler stared down at the picture. Her hair was longer and darker in it. He liked it. 'She'd have known they would come after her.' He looked up. 'But I don't understand. If she's dead, then how can she be back? You haven't found this glove-thing have you?'

'The glove was destroyed. That's not behind this. All Torchwood deceased were kept at the Hub. Suzie Costello's body would have been frozen in the vault, and that's where our lab rat John Blackman's body was found. The drawers were all smashed up down there and you can imagine the smell and state of the place. Her body must have fallen out of one of the drawers. We were looking for recoverable technology not checking that the dead were still dead, so we didn't do a body count.'

'Something woke her up,' Cutler said, 'and whatever it was, I think it's taking her over. These deaths aren't just a murder spree. Something is turning these people's brains to mulch.' He paused. 'And there's something else. Something really bad is coming. Something dark and endless and unimaginable. I know that sounds crazy, but I feel it. I've found myself opening and closing doors and drawers. I think I was trying to tell myself that a doorway has been opened, to somewhere terrible, and we need to close it before it's too late.'

Jackson stared at him. 'I feel it too. I've been dreaming. Hellish dreams. I've not dreamed anything like it in all my years.'

'We need to find her, and figure out what it is. I can't believe that she's doing all of this willingly.' It sounded lame and he knew it. Judging by the report in front of him, Suzie Costello was a psychopathic killer and there was no way round it. But he'd seen something else. A different side to her. Listening to himself, he wondered if he was as crazy as she was. Still, he wanted to hear her explanation for himself. He needed to try and understand what was going on with her.

His phone rang and he listened to Andy Davidson at the other end. 'We'll meet you there. Secure the building but be discreet. I don't want anyone going in until I get there.'

'What is it?'

'Her apartment. You coming?'

Commander Jackson nodded, and took one last glance at the picture in the file. 'Aren't you going to circulate her photo? In case anyone sees her?'

'I'm not putting anyone at risk like that, and to be honest, I don't want her alerted. Not until we've decided how best to play this.'

'You think she's at home?'

Cutler shook his head. 'Not a chance. But we might learn something.' He looked again at the picture. 'Maybe give this to one of your men to get to the airports. I don't want her knowing we're looking for her but at the same time, let's keep her in the country.'

Chapter Twenty-Eight

For a long moment, Cutler couldn't speak. *Let's go to yours. Mine's a right bloody mess.* Wasn't that what she'd said? Was that a little private joke to herself? The body tied to the bed had probably been handsome and toned once, but it was hard to tell now. The man stared upwards, his eyes still wide and glazed, and his mouth hung open slightly. His skin had mottled where the blood was now long settled and Cutler knew from experience that if they rolled him over, his back would be purple. The air stank of the beginning of decay. When had she killed this man? The night before they slept together? Who was this stranger?

The sheets were soaked with blood from where she'd cut him and his naked body was like a patchwork quilt with squares of skin cut away on his arms and legs and torso. She'd taken her time killing him, that was obvious, and, although there were blue edges that gave away the original colour of the sheets, the bed was now a slick mass of crimson where he had lost so much blood. His hands and feet were tied to the head and foot boards. Was that how she'd got him so helpless? Lured him in for some fun? Had she actually had sex with him first? And if so, why had she killed this man and not him? He thought about the water she'd probably drugged him with last night. Had her intention been to put him to sleep and then kill him quickly? Why hadn't she? Because she had feelings for him? Could someone capable of what had been done to the dead man on the bed even be capable of loving someone? It was like looking at the actions of a stranger.

Bloody footprints led from the bed to the window and then to the bathroom, and he followed her path. Make-up was strewn in disarray across the surfaces and there was still a wet patch on the floor where she'd got out of the shower.

'Sir?'

He turned to find Andy Davidson in the doorway. 'Yes?'

'Station just called. We can't get a trace on her phone. She's using some kind of blocking device on it. God knows what.'

'Great.' Cutler wasn't really surprised. 'You find anything here?'

'Nothing, really. Just a laptop which is clean and some clothes. Basics in the kitchen. Tea. Coffee. Milk. Some bread that's going stale.'

'And of course a mutilated corpse,' Cutler added. Tea and coffee and a corpse. It summed Suzie Costello up perfectly. Partly so normal, and partly bat-shit crazy. 'Get the computer to the tech boys and let them dig around in it. And then get a team here to get the body.' He'd had enough of looking at it and headed back to the sitting room. 'Where's Commander Jackson?'

Andy was staring down at his phone, his expression dark and distracted. Who was he thinking of calling? His mum? The boss? Cutler clicked his fingers, and the sergeant looked up suddenly. 'The Commander?' Cutler asked again.

'Sorry. Outside.' Andy put his phone away. 'One of his men just turned up. Looked quite freaked out. Said he needed to speak to him in private.'

'Did he now?' Cutler said, striding towards the front door. 'We'll see about that.'

He found them in the corridor below, heads close together, the Commander listening intently as the other man spoke, his hands animated.

'What's going on?' Cutler asked, glancing upwards for any smoke alarms and then lighting a cigarette. The sight of the dead man had added to the creeping dread that was consuming him like a cancer on the inside. Whatever was coming, the time they had to find it was running out. As if in support of his words, a siren blared in the distance. There was more chaos in the city.

Commander Jackson nodded at the thin man who wore an untidy suit rather than a uniform. 'Go on, Dr Holdt,' he said. 'Detective Inspector Cutler knows about Torchwood and what they did. In this current situation, we have no secrets from him.' He turned to Cutler. 'I didn't want your sergeant hearing anything unusual.'

'So, what *is* going on?'

'There's a manual monitoring device that Harkness and his team would use to detect any alien activity or use of alien technology. It showed—'

'Rift activity?' Cutler cut in.

'That's right.' Dr Holdt looked surprised. 'Well, we've got it working again and have been trying to make sense of its readings. There are a *lot* of readings. The thing is going haywire. There are major spikes at all the locations the dead bodies were found, but now it seems as if, alongside the spiking that we understand, there are these stranger readings. Almost anti-readings. As if whatever is happening there is so out of the machine's remit it can't compute them.' He looked nervously from the Commander to the policeman. 'And given that the machine's sole function is to register anything alien, then whatever it is must be very alien indeed.'

'Has anyone been to the locations of these weird readings?' Cutler asked.

'Yes, we sent a small team. There are black patches of something. Or maybe black patches of *nothing* would be more accurate. One of our men tried touching one and was sucked inside it. We've sent a couple of small probes in, and the readings go haywire until the probes are fully absorbed and then they go dead. The monitors still show that they're functioning but we can't get any readings. Whatever's on the other side is – appearances to the contrary – a long way away.'

'This is something to do with the Rift, though?' Cutler asked.

'Yes and no. Maybe something that once came through the Rift helped cause it, but our sources tell us that in the last hour NASA have been recording some kind of spatial disturbances but aren't giving any details – and I think that's because they *can't.*'

'Jesus.' The Commander had visibly paled. They were all out of their depth here, that much was clear, but Cutler reckoned that Jackson had it worst. The scientist's brain would be finding this fascinating as well as terrifying, and Cutler at least had come across alien activity twice before. For the Commander, even though he was in charge of the Hub site, this was a whole new world opening up.

This was a whole new world opening up. The phrase replayed in his head and hit him like a bucket of cold water. That was the terror. The awful dread. A whole new world – no, not a world – a *dimension* – was opening up.

'Something's trying to absorb the world,' he muttered. His hand trembled as he sucked hard on the cigarette. 'We're being pulled into the darkness.'

'That doesn't make sense,' Dr Holdt shook his head. 'We're getting no clear readings that would be expected from anything coming from space.'

'This isn't our known space. *This* shouldn't be here.' Cutler fought the panic that made him want to throw himself out of the nearest window rather than face what was coming for them.

'What about the people Sue Costa – Suzie Costello's been murdering?' Jackson asked. 'The ones with scrambled brains and no eyes. How do they tie in?'

Cutler's head throbbed. 'I'm not sure they're entirely dead.' *The screaming of millions.* 'Their bodies might be, but their consciousnesses? Their souls? I think they're in that other place. The one that's now spreading out in the dark patches and pulling people in whole. That's what it wants. Us.' He was right, and he knew it. He'd felt it, a slight tug just before he'd remembered the previous night. There had been something pulling at him and he now knew where it was coming from. 'We need to stop it. Now, before it's too late.'

'How?' Commander Jackson asked. 'How the hell do we do that?'

'Suzie Costello,' Cutler said. 'We need to draw her back to us. This started with her coming back to life in the Torchwood vault and there has to be some technology at the bottom of this. Something she's using. She killed your man there and hasn't stopped since. And I'm not talking about that poor sod back there in the bed. I mean the exploding-eyes victims. Given that she's clearly very bloody clever and she's been sitting in your office for days, I bet she knows that we're looking for her by now. Why has she kept on killing like that? Knowing that it'll draw attention to her and is also making the darkness stronger? She must know these dark patches all over the city are down to her. Why hasn't she stopped?'

Both of the other men stared at him. For people clearly experts in their respective fields, neither of them would have been any good as policemen.

'Because she *can't*,' he finished. 'And that's our hook.'

'Have you got a plan?' Jackson asked.

'Yes,' Cutler answered, nodding slowly. 'I think I do.' As he ground his cigarette out on the carpet he wished it had brought him some relief.

Chapter Twenty-Nine

After a while, not wanting to draw attention to herself, even though most people were avoiding coming near her, Suzie had taken refuge in the ladies' toilets. When she'd stood up and seen how her shadow stayed behind on the seat, she wasn't sure whether to laugh or cry some more. In the end, she chose crying.

Her phone had been ringing over and over, and she turned it off as she sat in the locked cubicle and rested her head against the wall. Quiet. She needed some peace and quiet so she could think. Try and find a way out of this.

Over the past twelve hours she'd felt everything start to crumble. Control was shifting. Was it because she'd let her guard down with her sudden rush of feelings for Cutler? Had the darkness inside sensed that and managed to somehow overpower her management of it? Or was this just the inevitable turn of events? She was still Suzie Costello, and she still wasn't quite as good as she thought she was. She *had* become Death – and so much more – but only because the vast awfulness behind her eyes had made it so. She was a puppet, nothing more.

Her head ached with the distant screams of those it had already taken. Not just the ones she'd *shown*, but others, people who had wandered into the driftwood of darkness that had broken away from her. She could feel those pieces, though, deep in her core wherever the device had gone to. They were still part of her and she part of it. What would happen to her when it had consumed the world, she wondered? Would it send her back to the nothingness of death or drag her into the agony with all the rest?

Her mouth twisted into a bitter smile and her eyes filled with tears again. Why could nothing go right for her? Where had the new Suzie gone to now? Where was all that confidence? She peeled more skin back from her fingernails as snot ran from her nose. This wasn't how it was supposed to be. Not at all. What was she supposed to do now? She should be long gone, and she'd probably left it too late. Cutler wasn't stupid and neither was that old buffoon Jackson. They'd know she wasn't who she claimed to be by now, even if they hadn't figured out exactly who she was. They'd have alerted the airports, if nothing else. It was all such a mess.

She winced as a fresh scream filled her head and then faded as the hell inside her took it. One more dark shadow she'd left behind somewhere serving its purpose.

'Just leave me alone,' she mumbled. 'Just take

them and leave me alone.' For an awful moment, she thought she heard laughter coming from the dimension that looked out on the world from within her tiny body. That was new. There had never been anything obviously sentient about it before. But now... now there was conscious malice there. The *things* that lived inside it were watching and learning and they were so, so hungry.

She rubbed her eyes and took in a deep, shaky breath. She needed to get a grip. There had to be a way out of this. There always was. She was Torchwood. The thought made her laugh and sob all over again. Jack Harkness, wherever he was, would have something to say about that. All her time of good service had been forgotten when the trouble with the Resurrection glove came along. And of course Miss close-to-bloody-perfect Gwen Cooper. Jack had liked her. Suzie had seen it. He'd liked Gwen Cooper more in that first couple of days than he'd liked Suzie in all the time they'd known each other. It was as if he'd always somehow known that Suzie would end up being damaged goods. She hiccupped out a short loud laugh. He wouldn't have been wrong, of course. But she would bet that he'd never have envisaged her as the one to cause the end of the world, and very probably the universe. What was inside her would consume it all, eventually, she was sure of that.

Suddenly the world, even the grubby inside of the station toilets, seemed beautiful. There was so much light and laughter and joy in it. Yes, there was pain and heartache and death, but there was so much more. It was all she'd ever wanted. To have a chance to enjoy that for longer. To *be* someone that mattered. Last night, she'd found someone that she mattered to and who could matter to her. Someone equally damaged. What would he think of her if he could see her now? If he could see what she'd done?

She turned her phone on again and stared at it. Had he given up calling? She hoped not. Did he hate her already? How much could he know? The phone beeped several times with answerphone messages, and then the text tone went off. She opened it. She couldn't help herself. It was from Cutler.

I know something alien is making you do this. I can help you. We can get out of this. Check the news. Meet me at the Hub at ten p.m. The vault. Trust me. Sounds stupid but I think I love you.

She stared at the message for what felt like an eternity before she realised her eyes had dried. It could be a trap. It was *probably* a trap. How could he help her? Surely, he just wanted to catch her? Still, her heart thumped rapidly, and as her hope grew she felt some small control over the darkness return. Somewhere, several of the dark patches that stained Cardiff disappeared and drew back inside her. It wasn't enough, but it was something. She needed to stay strong. She re-read the last two sentences over and over and then finally got to her feet. She needed to find somewhere with a TV.

Chapter Thirty

Back at the station, in a secure room, Elwood Jackson watched the news story unfolding on the screen. Even though he knew it was a fabrication, he still felt decidedly strange about it. Still, it had been approved by both his military and Department bosses, and to be honest they hadn't had a lot of choice. It *had* to be him to make it convincing. No one else would have had the access to either the systems or the equipment without being questioned. He was glad, however, that he didn't have a wife sitting at home, kept out of the loop of course, and watching this unfold. It was a lonely existence he'd chosen, but it had always been his belief that only selfish soldiers married and had families. Why would you burden anyone with so much potential grief? Today, he was pretty damned sure he was right in his thinking.

'Although the police are refusing to comment at this stage, it is believed that Commander Elwood Jackson, the official in charge of the excavation project on Roald Dahl Plass, has been arrested in connection with a series of murders that have

taken place in Cardiff over recent days. The police are taking control of the site, and all work there appears to have been suspended until further notice. This has once again raised concerns about the nature of the government facility destroyed in a terrorist attack last month. Dr David Jones, an eminent professor at Cardiff University's Department of Scientific Research, told reporters that, in light of the massive increase in reported suicides over the past forty-eight hours, some sort of mood-altering virus leak can't be ruled out...'

'You think she'll believe this?' Jackson asked as they switched the TV off.

'The key thing here is that she'll *want* to believe it. And that's half the battle won.' Cutler lit a fresh cigarette, despite the building being entirely non-smoking. It would appear that, for now, they were operating outside of normal rules. Saving the world clearly got some allowances made. As he watched the tendrils of smoke dancing up to the ceiling, Elwood Jackson was very tempted to ask for one himself.

'Don't talk to me about battles,' he muttered, making do with taking a deep breath of the scent of Marlboro Lights that filled the room. 'Those I can deal with.'

'Well, in my line of work, it's nearly always a psychological battle. Whatever is going on, I imagine she's going to want this to stop as much as we do. The Hub is somewhere she's familiar with – even in the state it's in, it's as close to a home as she's ever had. She'll feel safe there, and right now I think feeling safe is what she wants most of all.'

'You really think she'll turn up with the device?' Jackson had little understanding of women, but having seen Suzie Costello acting as normal as the next person while at the same time killing strangers with the device and then doing what she did to that man in her flat, he wasn't entirely convinced.

'I told her I loved her,' Cutler said. 'And told her to trust me.' The policeman's face darkened. 'I don't think anyone's told Suzie Costello they love her in a long time. She'll come. She's going to want my help.' He blew out a long stream of smoke. 'And if your scientists have the data right from the Hub then there's no reason our plan won't work. But just remember – if we're not out, you go ahead with what we've agreed anyway.'

'It's all taken care of,' Jackson said. DI Cutler might have had some strange experiences in his working life, but he had no idea about the tough calls Jackson himself had made over the years. 'If you're not out, that's it. Good luck.'

Cutler nodded. 'Thanks.' He reached for his coat. 'Well, I should probably get going. You'll have to stay here. I'll get someone in your uniform in the cells and your name logged in the system. Just in case she's got someone feeding her information from here. I wouldn't put it past her.'

'Take care, Detective.' The images from Jackson's nightmares surged in the darkness behind his eyes. Despite all his practicality and lack of imagination, he knew the policeman was right. Something terrible was coming. 'Can I ask you one thing?' he said. 'You don't have to answer.'

'Fire away.' Cutler was at the door, and he cut a lonely figure, heading off to save the world.

'Did you mean it? When you told her you loved her?' He didn't know why it mattered, but somehow it did.

Cutler looked at him for a long moment before answering. 'Yes. Yes, I meant it.' His eyes darkened. 'But it won't stop me doing my job, you can count on that.'

Elwood Jackson stood between Peters and Stand, the two Department men who'd arrived from London that afternoon. At least a whole brigade hadn't arrived. Perhaps they hadn't quite grasped the seriousness of the situation, but he thought these two at least were surely catching up now. They muttered to each other occasionally or turned their backs to quietly take phone calls that Jackson and his men clearly weren't supposed to hear. God only knew what they were relaying back.

Dr Holdt had joined them in the room up in the higher levels of the Millennium Centre, where they could look out through the glass windows between the huge letters to where the police now guarded the site.

'I hope you've understood the data correctly, Dr Holdt,' he said, softly. 'Or else, I do believe we're all in trouble.'

'Let's just hope the woman shows up,' Dr Holdt answered. He didn't sound quite as respectful as he had earlier in the day, and Jackson knew it was because he wasn't dressed in his full uniform. He was still the Commander though, and this was still his operation. Even if the Department were quietly coming up with their own back-up plan. Not that rank would really matter if that came to pass. 'So, the data you have definitely shows that there was alien activity present as soon as the building was destroyed?' he asked.

'Yes,' Holdt said. 'The monitor hadn't failed; we just weren't working it properly. The signal from the day of the explosion is weak and given everything else that was going on at that time there were lots of readings to work our way through, but there was definitely a slight spike of alien activity in the vault on that day. It stays almost invisible until the point when John Blackman was killed at which point the strength was much higher.'

Commander Jackson nodded. Cutler had better be right with his reasoning. If the explosion was what had started the device working, then an explosion should shut it down. All he needed to do was get it out of Suzie Costello's grip. If she thought that keeping the device close to her was keeping her alive, then Cutler was going to need all his persuasive charm. That worried Jackson. As far as he could see, Cutler didn't have that much. Still, as long as what he had worked on Suzie, that was all that mattered.

'Look,' Dr Holdt said, and something in his voice had all the men staring out of the window immediately. There she was, Sue Costa, or Suzie Costello or whatever other names she had on passports tucked away in safety deposit boxes across the country, slowly walking towards the Hub site. She had balls, Jackson had to give her that. But then, what else could you expect from a woman who'd been dead twice?

'Are the explosives ready?' he asked. At a desk in the far corner, a man hunched over a laptop nodded.

This was it then, Elwood Jackson thought. The fate of the world was now in Detective Inspector Tom Cutler's hands. He was surprised to find that he felt quite calm. He just had to roll with it. He'd live or die with the rest of them.

Chapter Thirty-One

'Given the increased damage levels of the current situation in Cardiff, I presumed that we'd be seeing the organ grinder rather than the monkey today,' Mr Black, the head of the Department said as he took his seat at the table, a cup of coffee in hand.

'Ha, bloody, ha. I have the full authority of the PM to chair this meeting on his behalf.'

Mr Black wasn't the only one to let out a slight snigger around the table. 'Yes,' one voice muttered, 'remind me to lose an election some time. Quickest way to the top these days.'

'Enough.' The butt of their jokes glared at each of the men and women around the table as he snapped the word. The group quietened, but more out of politeness than fear or respect. Most of them were faces entirely unknown by the general public – the real faces of power in the country, the kind of power that came from more than just oratory. 'We're all busy, so let's get to business, shall we? First, the PM wants to know what the situation is with the missing Torchwood personnel.' He looked over to a thickset woman to his right. 'I take it Harkness and Gwen Cooper are still unaccounted for? No signs of them at all?'

'Thus far, no. We have a cross-agency alert out –' several heads nodded in agreement – 'but we're not getting anything. Harkness, of course, may not even be on Earth, but we're hoping to find Cooper and her husband within the next few weeks.'

'Shouldn't be that difficult,' Mr Black cut in. 'She's pregnant, after all. At some point, she's going to be ready to push it out. She'll need medical care then.'

'And what about the items that have been recovered? Do we have any buyers for those yet?'

'We're weighing up the options,' Mr Black said. 'There are obviously security issues with buyer choice.' He nodded at a man and woman seated opposite. 'MI5 and MI6 are exploring the bidders.'

'The PM would like that hurried along. We're in a recession, and there's only so many cutbacks we can make before the cut is going to be running along our political throat, as it were. There's only so much we can blame the jobless scrounger element of society for. Soon it will be the jobseekers losing their allowances. We need a cash injection and quickly. The Americans seem the obvious choice as far as we can see.'

'Rich and stupid?'

'Something like that. Just make it happen and quickly.'

Mr Black's phone rang and he answered it. No

one questioned him. As he listened, he peered out of the Westminster window. The sky was grey and rain smeared the glass. Down below, people scurried here and there through London's streets. Cardiff seemed a million miles away.

'Thank you.' He ended the call. All eyes at the table stared at him.

'The situation in Cardiff is apparently somewhat worse than we originally thought. The men on the ground there are attempting to control it and we'll know shortly if they have. If they fail, however, we may need to consider more drastic action.'

'More drastic?' It was the head of MI6 that asked the question first.

Mr Black thought of the bustling city that had the misfortune to have been built below the Rift. 'Nuclear, in fact,' he said. 'We may need to destroy the city. Before whatever is happening there destroys the entire world.'

There was a long pause, during which time Mr Black sipped his coffee. Finally, the man at the head of the table, who had paled quite significantly since snapping at them for order, swallowed hard. 'I think we might need the PM himself for that kind of go-ahead,' he said eventually.

Even with the gravity of the situation, Mr Black had to fight a small smile.

Chapter Thirty-Two

He had followed the directions he'd been given and worked his way carefully through the wreckage of the Hub. Despite the portable fluorescent lamps that hung here and there on collapsed masonry or the remnants of walls, most of the site was filled with an eerie darkness. Tom Cutler breathed slowly and deeply to fight the rising panic that constantly threatened to overwhelm him.

He'd never suffered from claustrophobia, and nor was he particularly afraid of the dark – neither of those would be good traits for a detective – but down here it was almost as if the terrible blackness Suzie was spreading had come to find him. He knew that wasn't true – this was just ordinary darkness – but in the quiet, with only his shuffling movements and the occasional drip of water from somewhere on site it was hard not to let the dread inside take over. Instead he tried to picture the place as it was when he had last been there.

As he passed under tumbling networks of wires, he could almost see Ianto Jones standing behind a workstation, a coffee in his hand, staring up at a screen. Somewhere over there was Jack Harkness's office and that mess of concrete over to his right had collapsed into a cavernous hole that might be the wreckage of the Boardroom where he'd sat among them and planned how to trap the alien that was murdering the best singers in Wales.

How strange that they'd never mentioned Suzie, he thought, as he picked his way down to the next level of darkness in the bowels of the building. But then they'd barely mentioned their two colleagues who'd only just died. Was that how it was for Torchwood? Always moving forward? Was losing their workmates just part of the job? People talked about it in policing, but it was rare. This wasn't America, where officers lost their lives in shootouts with drug lords, and Cutler wasn't convinced it happened over there all that much. He thought of Gwen Cooper, ex-uniformed officer, then Torchwood, and now what? Was she somewhere amongst the dead down here? The maudlin turn of his thoughts didn't help the fear in his core, *the screaming of millions* that was coming if they couldn't stop it.

He trod more carefully now, aware that not only was the site still a danger zone of its own making, but that earlier that afternoon, Army bomb experts in police uniforms had come in and planted several packages of explosives in key structural areas around him. It was hard to imagine what a key structural area might be in all this mess, but he trusted those men to have found them. Once Suzie arrived – *if* Suzie arrived – then he had half an hour to get her to give up the technology and get them both out of there before the place went up. Or came down, depending on how you looked at it. Either way, whatever was left of the Hub would be blasted to dust.

The vault was cool, the air filled with a vaguely sickly smell that he didn't want to ponder on and he refused to look over at the crumpled bank of drawers, some of which would have held alien artefacts, and the rest – well – somewhere in there must be the crushed dead bodies of Toshiko Sato and Owen Harper and whoever else had died in the name of Torchwood. Strips of blue light were dotted here and there, and he scanned the space with his torch to get his bearings. If he couldn't get Suzie to leave the device behind for whatever reason, then he was going to have to keep her down here until the bombs blew. He was surprised by the calm practicality of the thought – the summation of his own possible death. Perhaps he just wasn't really accepting it. Or maybe, and he thought this was the more likely cause of his pragmatism, he could feel that his life, woven as it had been with Torchwood for so long, had been leading up to this point. Perhaps this was his purpose.

He almost laughed at the Zen quality his thinking had taken on. Sometimes he was so full of shit. What would happen would happen, but he was pretty damned determined to get out of it alive. He sat down on the upturned metal drawer that lay half-exposed under some rubble.

He laid his torch down on the floor, idly noting an unfamiliar name stencilled on an empty packing crate: 'Colasanto'. He pulled out a cigarette. Sod being told not to. If there was gas down here, there'd have been an explosion already. The yellow flash of his lighter was warm in the gloom, and he left it open for a few seconds longer as he sucked in the smoke. That was better. Right now, cigarettes were hardly top of the league for things likely to kill him. He stared into the golden flame and waited.

When his phone rang in the silence, he almost jumped out of his skin. *Suzie* – that was his first thought. She wasn't coming. She'd seen through their plan.

'Yes?' he said softly.

'I need you to give Suzie a message for me,' the voice at the other end said.

Cutler froze, his heart thumping. American. Smooth. Determined. 'Jack?' he said. 'Jack Harkness?'

'Tell Suzie I'm coming for her.'

'Jack? What –?' The phone went dead in his ear. Captain Jack bloody Harkness. Of course. Cutler's face flushed angrily. Who the hell was he to turn up now – at the last minute when all the work had been done. He looked at the rubble around him that hid the powerful explosives. 'You might be too late to come for her this time, Captain Jack.'

It was about twenty minutes and three cigarettes later that Cutler heard movement. Footsteps, light and delicate, carefully making their way through the wreckage towards him. When she stepped into the remains of the vault, the soft hues of the unnatural light tainted her skin. Was this how she'd looked when she was dead, he wondered? Ethereal blue? No, he dismissed it. Right now, standing awkwardly a few metres away from him, she looked beautiful. The dead never did, no matter how much you dressed them up and rouged their cheeks. The best you got was a strange-looking waxwork dummy. Suzie Costello had been shot several times before she'd died the second time round, and the first time she'd put a bullet through her own brain. Even with her looks, her corpse would not have been pretty.

'So,' he said softly, 'I've managed to park the blame on Jackson for now, but it won't last. This thing is out of control.'

She laughed a little, and then it turned into a sob and his heart ached. 'You could say that.'

She didn't move towards him, but he could see her eyes glistening as they darted this way and that.

'How much do you know?' she asked. She couldn't meet his gaze.

'Enough,' he said. 'For now, at least.' He tapped the space beside him, and she crept forward a couple of steps but didn't sit. 'I ran a test on a hair on my shirt and it matched those left at crime scenes which linked to the deleted file.' He kept his voice soft and even. 'So I'm guessing you're Torchwood. Just not of the Torchwood team I met.

I'm not quite sure what you came back here for,' he looked around at the wreckage, 'but you did for whatever reason, and then you found the activated device and took it with you. And now it's making you kill people, and I think it has plans for all of us? How am I doing, honey?'

He lit another cigarette. They were completely apart from the world down here in the earth, and it was hard to think of all those dead people, and that mutilated man in her flat, and link them with this fragile woman in front of him, whose smell he could still remember. He thought of Captain Jack Harkness's message. *Tell Suzie I'm coming for her.* Well, this time round he wasn't doing what Jack Harkness dictated. Whatever was going on down here, it was between him and Suzie. He was taking care of it. He didn't need Jack to get involved.

She stared at him for a long moment. 'Did you mean it when you said you loved me?' It was a child's voice. As if, even in this situation, love was the only thing that mattered.

'Yes, I did.' He looked into her dark eyes. 'I think you're messed up and I don't know what is going on in your head, but yes, I love you. I feel *right* with you. I'm hoping we can get this situation sorted and see if that's real.' He meant it, even though he knew it was a lie. If they got out of here alive, then Suzie had other crimes to answer for. There was no way he was going to be able to whisk her away into the sunset.

Her tears breaking free in streams down her

face, she sat down heavily beside him and rested her head on his shoulder. 'Why couldn't I have met you years ago?' she whispered. 'Before the glove. Before everything started to go wrong?'

'Life just doesn't work that way.'

She hiccupped a small laugh. 'I'm an expert on life and death. Death especially. Not just killing people. I've *been* there.' He wiped a tear from her cheek. It was so warm, so alive, and she looked so sweet. 'You don't understand,' she said, looking away. 'I didn't come back down here. I *was* down here.' The bitter tone made her voice deeper. 'I was in this drawer in fact. Dead. Nothing. And then suddenly I was alive again.'

'You were dead?' Cutler feigned surprise, but his heart warmed. She was telling him the truth and he couldn't help but feel happy about that, even though he was aware of their minutes ticking away and the need to get to the point.

'Twice.' She laughed again. 'God, it sounds so ridiculous.' She sniffed loudly. 'I wish I'd stayed dead.'

'I'm glad you didn't.'

She nestled in to him, the two of them like ghosts in the gloom, as he smoked. 'The device brought me back to life I think. When it activated. It healed me.'

'We need to destroy it,' Cutler said, pulling away so he could look at her. 'You know that, don't you?'

'It scares me,' she said. 'It's so much stronger than me and I can't control it any more. I'm leaving bits of it behind.'

'I know. But we can turn it off. Why haven't you destroyed it already? Are you scared of what that will do to you? Don't be, you look pretty healed to me.'

'It's not that simple,' she said.

'Why?' he asked. 'Is it like some kind of drug? Has it got you hooked?' He frowned. She wasn't carrying a bag. 'Where is it anyway?'

'It's inside me,' she said, simply, her eyes full of dread. She lifted her shirt, exposing her smooth, flat stomach. 'I had it sewn into the other side of my skin before all this started. Before my *first* death. I thought it might make the glove stronger. When the Hub collapsed, the energy must have activated it and it brought me back to life. I could see it under there – a flashing red light – just like when Tosh made it work after we found it on the beach.' She looked up at him. 'But now it's gone. It's still working, but I think it's right inside me somewhere. Somewhere I won't be able to get at it.' Her dark eyes had filled with tears again. 'I don't know what to do. I thought I had everything under control. I thought I'd been so *clever*.' She wiped her nose. 'I just want it to stop. I can hear them screaming.'

The screaming of millions. Cutler's mind raced as a chill settled through him. What did they have? Ten minutes at the most to get out and leave the device behind.

'It's all right. We'll get it out of you.' He barely heard his own words. What would happen if he called Jackson? Would they get a medical team in and take the time to try and save Suzie before destroying the device? No. They'd just blow the place up anyway. The butt of the cigarette burned his fingers and he dropped it. They'd be right as well. The fate of the entire world depended on destroying the device.

'It's so far inside me,' she said again. 'I think it's in my heart or my lungs. It's bedded into me. As if it's part of me.'

'I'll call a medical team.' He was glad of the gloom. He'd never been a good actor and he didn't want her to see the pain on his face. He'd found her and now he was going to lose her again. There was no way he could save her. Not now. There just wasn't enough time. He pulled out his phone and dialled his own home number knowing she'd hear the ringing tone, and then got up and moved towards the entrance to the vault, speaking into his answerphone, demanding someone send an ambulance immediately. He clicked off the call and turned back to face her. 'They'll be here in ten minutes,' he said. 'I'll go up and keep an eye out for them. You stay here. My men think you're down here helping me with the Jackson investigation anyway. I'll only be a couple of minutes.'

'Don't leave me down here, Tom,' she said. 'Please.'

He stared at her. Five more minutes until the bombs would go off. Commander Jackson would be staring at the entrance to the Hub and willing him to come out. Either him or both of them. He fought the temptation to take her upstairs with him and make a run for it. He wanted her to live, he wanted them both to live, but at what cost? The entire planet? All those people he'd vowed to protect? He couldn't do it. And could he live with himself if he left her down here, alone? There was no more memory drug to take to wipe her out, and he didn't think he would even if he could. She fascinated him. Good, bad or otherwise, there was something in her that called out to him.

'OK,' he said and then smiled softly. 'Kiss me.'

'Even after all this trouble?' she said. 'You still want me?'

'Now more than ever.' There was no lie in that, even if she wouldn't understand why until it was too late.

Somewhere in the corner of his eye he saw a small red light appear. The explosives were arming. They were out of time.

'Come here, gorgeous,' he said.

He held her face in his hands and had his lips on hers as the first surge of energy blasted through the small space. Light filled the vault as balls of white flame raced to meet each other as each explosion went off.

Tom Cutler was amazed at how much could happen in such a small nanosecond of time. *This is it*, he thought. *My death coming for me.* As the breath was knocked from their lungs, Suzie pulled away from their kiss, her dark eyes wide and her mouth in an O.

He held her arms tightly. 'I love you,' he thought he said.

'No,' she whispered.

In that briefest of moments, he thought perhaps she didn't love him at all, and he was dying for nothing, and then he wondered if perhaps she was railing against a third death, and then, in the last fraction of the second when her eyes changed colour and the terrible darkness was so clear in them, he knew that her 'no' was for him. The darkness was taking her with it, and she didn't want it to take him too.

He heard the screams. He saw her terror. And he refused to look away.

Their bodies burned.

Epilogue

On top of the Millennium Centre, a dark figure stood staring down at the lights and activity taking place in what was left of the Hub. He was a mere strip of shadow against the starry night, and he remained motionless as he waited for the confirmation he needed from below. He'd stood here night after night since the second round of explosions, ignored by those who were so focused on finding what was lost beneath the ground that they had forgotten to look up occasionally. He frowned a little as, below, the old and weary Commander followed a soldier back to the enclosed area. Perhaps this was it.

'We've found them, sir.'

It was 3 a.m., and Commander Elwood Jackson – retired Commander as soon as this job was brought to its grim conclusion – was exhausted. They'd been working for over a week now, digging to find the bodies. It was at least quicker than the first excavation at the site had been. Whereas then the hunt had been a delicate process, wanting to preserve as much as possible of the equipment and technology, this time round it was simply to dig down to the vault and find some evidence of Tom Cutler and Suzie Costello's deaths.

He'd told the Department men that they needed to be absolutely sure that she and the technology that had brought the darkness were both destroyed and they had gone along with that. He knew they were just humouring him slightly, but given that Cardiff had returned to normal – there were no more black patches, nor any suicides – they would give him two weeks to find what he was looking for and then, after that, the site would be filled in, and the whole mess forgotten. They'd got all the technology they needed anyway. For Jackson's part, he preferred not to dwell on the alien devices. He'd had enough of those.

'There's not much to see,' the soldier said as Jackson followed him to the covered tarpaulin area. 'They were at the heart of the explosion. Their bodies were pulverised together. It's hard to tell which bit comes from one and which from the other.'

Jackson wondered if the man had ever lost a friend. DI Tom Cutler had sacrificed himself to save them all, and this youngster was talking about him as if he were nothing. He found that he was glad that he'd be leaving the Army. He'd seen enough callousness to last several lifetimes.

'I just want to see his face,' he muttered.

'We have the upper portions of both their heads. Obviously messy, but they must have been standing facing each other.'

Jackson pushed past him while he was still speaking and headed to the tables that were covered with parts of bodies mixed with bits of concrete. Here and there he saw a flash of fabric that at one time had been clothing.

'They're under that cloth,' the soldier said softly. He didn't follow Jackson over. Maybe he had some compassion after all.

Elwood Jackson pulled the sheet back. For a long while he stared. First at the wrecked face and missing eyes of the woman he'd known as Sue Costa, and then over at DI Tom Cutler. Even in the unrecognisable mess of his face, it was clear that the policeman's eyes were gone.

'You couldn't let her go alone, could you?' he said. 'You stupid, brave bastard. You couldn't let her go alone.'

For the first time in a very long time, Elwood Jackson wondered if he might cry. He didn't. Instead he swallowed his tears and drew himself up tall carefully covering over the pitiful remains.

'That's all I wanted to see,' he barked at the soldier as he passed. 'The site can be filled.'

From the top of the building, the dark-haired man watched the Commander as he left the site, his shoulders slumped. The old man paused for a second, out of view of his command, and then leaned his head back to suck in a deep breath of the night air. He rubbed his hands over his face. He walked away from the site and didn't look back. The Commander didn't notice either the man at the top of the building, or the pale-haired police sergeant who stood watching the demolished site, his shoulders hunched with the burden of knowledge. Eventually, Andy Davidson also turned and walked away from the wreck of the Hub.

Watching him, Captain Jack Harkness smiled softly. It was a sad smile, but a satisfied one. He turned away. His part here was over.

The darkness that settled over Cardiff held no shadows and unnatural places, and this time the city slept. For most, the hours passed peacefully, as if on some unconscious level the population were aware of the escape they'd had and were lost in relief.

It wasn't like that for the Commander. That night, and for so many nights afterwards, when Elwood Jackson dreamed, it wasn't the screaming of millions that haunted him, but the screaming of one man, forever lost in Hell. When he woke, sweating into his sheets, he realised how very relieved he would be when there was only a quiet nothing waiting for him after death.

Acknowledgements

As usual, a big thank you to my editor, Steve Tribe, for giving me this gig, and for always being there with his encyclopaedic and awe-inspiring knowledge of all things *Torchwood* when I needed a quick answer to a question.

A second thanks to him and to Russell T Davies and the powers that be in Cardiff for letting me give Suzie Costello one last adventure. I loved her in the show, and totally loved bringing her back from the dead. Bad girls rock.